JACK

A FOLK HORROR TALE

TWISTED TALES

R. P. HOWLEY

DANIEL WILLCOCKS

DEVIL'S
ROCK

OTHER TITLES BY DEVIL'S ROCK PUBLISHING

Twisted Tales Series

Jack

Heir

Slay

Deal

Novels

Dream

The Hotel

When Winter Comes

Anthologies

Bolts of Fiction

The Omens Call

The Other Side

Keep up-to-date at

www.devilsrockbooks.com

A SPECIAL THANKS TO OUR ARC READER TEAM

Billie, Emily Haynes, John Shields, Kiz Moncrieff, Luka Jae, Luke Kondor, Pat Eroh, Terry.

This book wouldn't be what it is without your encouragement, kind words, and support. You guys rock.

For Stine, King, and every other titan of horror who paved the way so we could tread these twisted, cobbled streets.

JACK

CHAPTER

ONE

It all started so quickly. The attack of the pumpkins.

Charli Clarke didn't see it coming. Not the flashes of orange. Not the twin cackles of laughter. Not the excitement etched onto the two swollen, orange faces or the rushing bodies barreling toward her.

Her gaze was glued to the screen of her phone, bright and luminous in the dark night.

"*Jack! You're it. Ha-ha!*"

Charli managed only a short, sharp gasp before she was knocked to the ground. The phone slipped from her hand. It landed heavily beside her, smacking against the frigid cobbles.

The screen went black.

"You monsters!"

Charli turned to see the pair of kids, complete with makeshift pumpkin heads bobbing on skinny shoulders, sprinting away from her, legs and arms flailing.

"Sorry!" one yelled back.

"Tag, you're it!" yelled the other.

Charli growled.

"Babe, are you OK?" Nate Bradley appeared from around the trunk of the car, luggage forgotten. He scooped Charli with muscular arms, the musk of his scent from a long car journey already working to soothe Charli's anxiety. His engagement ring, the one she'd chosen oh-so carefully, glinted in the light of the moon, pregnant but not quite full.

His forehead creased, even as he tried to hide a wry smile. "What the hell was that?"

Before Charli could reply, a woman jogged up to them. Her hair showed the first signs of gray, matching the bags beneath her eyes that betrayed her exhaustion. She doubled over, gasping, then placed doughy hands on motherly hips. A sparkling gold watch shone proudly on her wrist, seeming out of place with the rest of her Plain Jane attire. "I'm right in guessing you've just had an encounter with my two scarecrows?"

Charli looked down the street, the pumpkin heads nowhere in sight. "Is that what they were? I've got a few other things I'd like to call them—"

"Babe!"

"But don't worry, I won't."

The woman let out a shuddering sigh. She glanced nervously over her shoulder, her words quick and frantic. "I'm so, so sorry. They're my little terrors. Lord, give me strength." She half-shrugged. "Single mama. Don't worry, they'll receive a suitable punishment."

A car door slammed shut. Charli's long-suffering twin brother, Alex, emerged from the driver's side.

"Dudes... What the hell? Oh, hey." Alex offered a wary smile. "I knew Brackenholt was famous for its pumpkins, but I've never seen one come alive before—let alone two." Alex's smile slipped when Nate glowered in his direction.

2

"Yeah, they're getting into the spirit early," the woman said. "Playing 'Jack' before the harvest moon hits."

"Playing... 'Jack'?" Alex asked.

The woman waved a placating hand. Somewhere in the distance they heard a woman's scream, followed by the shouts of an angry man. "Just one of our small-town customs. An urban legend." Another cry, followed by boys' laughter. "Christ. I'm sorry, I've got to neuter the bulls."

With that, she tore down the quaint village street as fast as her legs could carry her, rushing by small cottages, thatched roofs, and dark windows, a slight limp that made her run crooked with every step.

"Not the best start to our weekend, huh?" Nate said, examining Charli for any signs of hurt. "Are you OK? No broken bones, no blood loss, no need for emergency surgery? I'll be honest, I'm not sure where the hospital is in this backwater village."

"If they even have one," Alex added.

"I'm fine. I told you this was a stupid idea," Charli pawed at her eyes, exhaustion settling in after a long.eight-hour trip—a trip she hadn't even wanted to come on. But how could she turn down the offer of adventure and excitement that filled her two favorite men's eyes when they'd invited her? After all, with Nate's promised promotion looming, who knew how much quality time they were going to have together after Halloween?

"Look, stop fussing." She pulled herself out of Nate's grasp, scanning the ground for her phone. "Shit." She scooped it up, a spider web crack covering the screen. "*Fuck*. It won't even turn on. Seriously? Could tonight *get* any worse? I've been searching for signal for the last twenty miles, now I can't even *attempt* to speak to my friends?"

Nate grimaced and looked to Alex for help.

"Look," Alex said, "it could be worse. You could be standing there with the knowledge that there *is* a signal, but you can't connect to it?"

Nate rolled his eyes. "For fuck's sake. Really?"

"What?" Alex held up his hands. "I'm trying, OK? I'm not the one that got attacked by jack-o'-lantern-demon-spawn the moment we stepped out of the car. Don't take this out on me."

Nate sighed. "Let's just get our things inside, yeah? We need to get settled and get our bearings. Anyway, we've already driven all this way, and—"

"We?" Alex said with a smirk. "Who's this we? I'm the one who—"

Charli snorted. "Well, you wouldn't let us take turns. That's your fault, bro."

"And why do you think that is?" Alex ran a caressing hand over the hood of the gleaming blue Mazda. "She's *my* pretty baby. Ain't nobody rides her like her daddy does."

Charli put two fingers in her mouth and retched. Nate laughed, wrapping an arm around Charli's shoulder and kissing her forehead. They stared at Alex expectantly.

"What?" Alex asked.

"Your punishment for swearing at my injured fiancé: you can get the bags."

Alex flipped the bird.

Nate ignored him. "We'll go get checked in. Crack on, mate. We don't want to miss our dinner reservation."

"Are you joking?"

"Doesn't look like it, does it?"

Nate led Charli across the street, leaving the stunned Alex behind. The old hotel loomed before them as Alex grumbled and opened the trunk. With each step toward the ancient building, Charli's trepidation grew. The hotel looked nothing like the one Alex and Nate had shown her online. The digital crop of the picture on lastminutebreaks.com must have been taken at least thirty years ago, before the building had invited thick ropes of ivy to snake around its base and walls.

The windows were grimy, the pillars—bleached white in the images—were a mottled gray, and as they walked through the entryway the building had a smell that reminded Charli of midsummer elementary school assemblies in packed wooden halls.

"Charming." Charli sighed.

"Oh, come on, babe. Give this a go, please. I know it's not quite what you're used to, but we can still have a good time together."

"Yeah. You, me, and *him*." She nodded to where Alex was struggling with the bags. Every time he picked up one, another would roll out of his arms and into the street.

"Moron."

"He's *your* twin brother. You can't hate him that much?"

"Can't I?" Charli stopped in the middle of the reception area. "I've spent my whole life with him. *We* barely get time alone together." She trailed two fingers from Nate's chin to his chest. "I thought we'd finally have some 'us' time. Me and you. Y'know, before it all changes."

Nate smiled sweetly. "And we'll have that, I promise. After picking pumpkins all day he'll be too exhausted to do anything else. We can go out for dinner and then spend the evenings in bed. How does that sound?"

Charli wanted to believe him, but if past experiences had shown her anything, it was that his plan fell onto the 'unlikely' side of the possibility scale. "But he's your best friend. I've seen how you two are together. He's not going to leave you alone."

Nate kissed Charli softly. "He's not going to have a choice. Me and you, babe. Promise."

"Promise?"

"Double promise."

They kissed, Charli's arms trailing their way around Nate's shoulders. She lost herself in the softness of his lips, the fluttering in her stomach that always accompanied physical contact with Nate enough to shave off a little apprehension. Maybe it would be OK. Maybe she could survive this weekend. It wouldn't quite be the romantic getaway she had hoped for, but perhaps she could have some fun along the way.

"*A-hem.*"

Charli and Nate broke their kiss to find Alex standing less than a foot from them both, eyes narrowed. "I thought you lovebirds were checking in, not filming a country porno."

Nate's neck flushed. Charli's face hardened. "Come on, babe. Let's check in so we can finally find a room with a lock."

"Ew, gross." Alex huffed as the three made their way to the vacant reception desk.

Ding!

Nate jumped. "Easy, tiger."

Charli raised her hand from the bell on the counter. "What? We've been here for ages, and—"

"It's been three minutes—"

"And nobody's come to help us."

Ding!

Ding!

Nate grabbed Charli's wrist. "Enough."

"Yeah, Cee-Cee. Listen to lover boy."

Charli glared at Alex. Alex smirked back.

Shuffling footsteps announced the arrival of an old man from the doorway behind the counter. He was tall—alarmingly so—and gangly, with a lean to his walk. The last of his hairs were cobwebs, clinging desperately to the smooth surface of his liver-spotted dome. Half-moon glasses perched on the tip of his nose. "May I help you?"

Nate reached into his pocket and slipped some folded pages across the counter. "Here to check in. One single room and one double."

A raised eyebrow was the only response. The man labored over examining the pages. With each passing second, Charli found her skin growing tight, a chill in the air pricking her body in goosebumps.

"Of course," the clerk replied at last. He turned to a small cabinet on the wall, the hooks bedecked with jangling keys.

"It's not even swipe cards?" Alex whispered. "What backwater hellhole did we just time travel to?"

"Shut up," Nate hissed. "Don't be so rude."

"You're here for the harvest?" the old man asked without looking, struggling to find the required keys for the rooms they'd booked.

"Yeah," Nate said, taking the volunteer role of making meaningless small talk. "We hear amazing things about your pumpkins. The largest in the county, or so the internet says. It's supposed to be character building, you know, helping in the fields and all that."

The clerk finally found the keys. He hooked two sets on his gnarled finger and turned slowly. He placed them on the counter under the cup of his hand and stood there smiling at them. "Oh yes, it's going to be a bountiful harvest this year."

"Is that right??" Alex said.

"I'm sure of it." The old man's eyes glinted.

Charli looked away, unable to hold his stare.

Nate shifted his weight to his other foot. "Why's that?"

The old man's lips twisted into a pained smile, as though his face had forgotten how to be authentically joyful. "It's a full Harvest Moon, this year. Fancy that? A *full* Harvest Moon on Halloween. Rare and blessed are these days."

"What's a harvest moon?" Charli asked, curiosity getting the better of her.

The old man blinked. Once. "When the moon is at its fullest. A spectacle to behold. Hues of red and orange. It means our workers can toil late into the night, bringing in a yield that flourishes larger compared to the moon's weaker phases. There's magic in the air and, oh, we are blessed. Oh, yes."

"Wait," Alex waved a hand, wedging himself between Charli and Nate, much to Charli's chagrin. "You're saying that the pumpkins grow larger, *because* of the moon?"

The old man ran a withered tongue across his dry lips, revealing several blackened teeth. "Yes. That and... well... Jack, of course. You think you've tasted those delicious fruits before now, but you haven't tasted anything yet." Keeping one hand clamped on the keys, he reached beneath the counter and rattled something out of sight. When his hand emerged, it contained a dozen blanched pumpkin seeds. He popped several into his mouth and began chewing wetly. A couple fell to the floor, clicking as they bounced. "There ain't nothing sweeter. This will be *the* year. Jack's harvest will be bountiful..." He swallowed and then beamed. Mashed seeds stained the gaps between broken piano teeth. He extended an arm to Charli. "Here."

Charli's hands clapped automatically to her mouth. "No thank you."

The old man beamed, eyes flashing at Charli's rejection.

Nate moved past Alex, positioning himself in front of Charli. "No offense. She doesn't like the taste of pumpkins. It's a whole thing."

"One of many," Alex chimed in.

Nate flashed a glare. "One I happen to adore."

The old man's smile grew wider, a rictus grin that wrinkled his cheeks and somehow seemed to make him grow. His eyes fixed on Charli, shoulders broadening. He appeared to swell before them as the air grew colder around them.

"It's nothing personal," Charli said defensively, attempting to break the strange intensity that filled the old man's face. "Just not for me. I don't like pears, either. Come to think of it, I've got a strange thing with fruit. Not sure where it comes from. Maybe it was my mom, or…"

She trailed off as the old man remained silent, unblinking. Nate and Alex exchanged a glance before Alex slowly leaned forward and slid his hand beneath the old man's.

Alex peeled the keys from their bony cage. "We'll take those, thanks." He quickly examined the fobs. "Rooms 107 and 108, right? Sweet. Thank you so much for your hospitality. Up there? Good."

"Yes, thank you," Charli added before they turned and scurried up the broad, carpeted staircase toward the upper levels.

She shuddered, feeling the man's gaze on her long after they were out of sight.

"What the hell was that about?" Alex asked as they combed the door numbers. "What a creep!"

"Keep your voice down," Nate said. "We don't know if they're listening on CCTV."

"CCTV? There aren't any cameras, Nate. CCTV didn't exist in 1905. It looks like Brackenholt hasn't even discovered electricity yet. What are you worried about?"

"That was weird, right?" Charli asked nervously. "Like, really weird. Like... what's wrong with not liking pumpkins? *You* don't like candy corn."

Alex scoffed. "Who does?"

Nate shrugged. "I suppose an old guy like that might find it weird for a volunteer picker to drive halfway across the country to spend a weekend picking something they despise the taste of."

Charli stopped. "This *wasn't* my first choice, Nate. Remember?"

Alex held up his hands. "Now, now. Before you guys get into a full-blown domestic, you should know two things."

"What?" Charli hissed.

"One: whatever you're about to argue about, it's not my fault."

Nate opened his mouth to protest.

"And *two*," Alex interjected. "These're our rooms."

Charli hadn't even noticed. The two rooms faced each other in the corridor. Charli's stomach knotted, realizing that no matter what she and Nate got up to, Alex would be within hearing range.

"Here." Alex dropped the keys for 107 into Nate's palm. "Meet again in ten minutes? Freshen up? Grab some food?"

"Sounds good." Nate refused to meet Charli's gaze as Alex closed the door behind him. He slid the key in the lock and twisted. The door swung open.

Charli's jaw dropped, and a silent scream escaped her lips.

CHAPTER
TWO

Charli stared at the atrocity. "What the fuck *is* that?"

Nate exploded into laughter. "Oh man, that's adorable."

Resting on the pillows of their double bed, a large jack-o'-lantern beamed at them. It had been carved with rough hands, the edges of the squinting eyes and too-wide mouth tattered with strings of flesh. Inside, the abhorrent head was hollow, except for the flickering flame of a small candle.

"Adorable?" Charli's eyes narrowed as she glared at Nate. "What kind of sicko leaves a decapitated head on the guests' beds? Is this some kind of Mafia hotel?"

"It's Halloween weekend, babe." Nate lowered his bags to the floor. "It must be tradition here or something."

Charli's nose wrinkled as she sniffed the air and tried to hold back the bile rising in her throat. "It's disgusting is what it is—not to mention a fire hazard."

She stared for a moment at the head, the creepiness of its hewn face sending shivers down her spine. The way the

11

candle played with the light inside those large, hollow eyes was dizzying, holding her attention despite her discomfort.

Alex ran into the room, stopping short behind the pair. "I heard a scream? And not the good kind."

Nate snorted and pointed at the bed.

"Oh." Alex chuckled, then tossed a handful of something into his mouth, chewing loudly. "Same over in mine. Nice little welcome package, huh? Very festive. Not sure who carved them, but if I were to put bets on it, probably those kids, Cee-Cee."

Charli shivered again and looked around the room, for the first time noticing the small bags and bowls that lined a nearby dressing table. There were bright orange bags of a variety of pumpkin-themed treats. Blanched, roasted, and spiced seeds, cling-filmed segments of pie—even a few packets of Reese's snack-sized peanut butter pumpkins.

"We really hit the jackpot, huh?" Alex managed, speaking with his mouth full as another handful of seeds passed his lips. "Soft bed. Warm place. Free food. You'll get no complaints from me."

"Shocking. You're going to ruin your appetite," Nate said, all the while studying Charli's face, spotting how pale she had turned. "Can you give us a few minutes? Please?"

"You sound just like Mom." Alex shrugged. "Fine. No more screaming though." He placed a hand on his chest. "My heart just can't take it."

When Alex closed the door, Nate approached the bed. He grabbed the pumpkin's stubby stalk and blew a sharp puff of air to extinguish the candle. The light sputtered and died, leaving a slightly modified scent of extinguished birthday candles.

"There. All gone. You're safe now."

Charli wrapped her arms around her body. "I doubt it.

The face is still there. And it friggin' stinks." She stared at her feet. "I don't know if I can do this."

Nate crossed the room and wrapped his arms around Charli's waist. "It's OK, I promise. Just a small bump at the start of the road. I'll shove this in Alex's room, and we'll air out this one, yeah?" He looked down, lifted her chin with a finger to meet her gaze. "We'll see if we can grab some scented candles on the way back from dinner, too? Make it all romantic. How's that sound?"

"But…"

"I want this to be fun for us, babe. We can still make the best of this weekend, can't we?"

Charli looked into Nate's green eyes. There had always been something about them that magnetized her, as though she were staring into the middle of a tropical lake. Even growing up, when Alex and Nate would spend hours locked in Alex's room playing *Tomb Raider III* and chain-eating Doritos, Charli would wait for those stolen moments when she would bump into Nate in the hall and catch a glimpse.

"Fine." She offered a weak grin. "Thank you."

He reached down, kissed her gently. Her skin grew warm as her fingers laced behind his neck. She raised herself onto her toes, pressing closer, their kiss growing more feverish. After a moment, she pulled away, her forehead resting on his. "You know… we could always skip dinner."

She grinned, enjoying the conflict that played across Nate's face. She loved the effect she had on him, the way she could press his buttons and tease.

"Charli…" He breathed deeply, eyes closed.

She kissed under his chin. "Come on. Where's your

sense of adventure?" Her hand slid down to the buckle of his belt.

"Charli... I... God, it's not that I don't want to... It's just..." Before Nate could finish his sentence, there was a loud knock on the door.

"Come on, lovebirds. Alex is getting hangry!"

Charli's shoulders dropped. Her lust faded to a prickly disappointment as Nate whispered beneath his breath, then reluctantly turned his head to the door. "Just a minute."

"Dude, I know what *that* means." The sounds of fake hurling came muffled through the wood. "That's my sister, bro."

Charli rolled her eyes and gently shoved Nate back. "We're done."

"Come on, babe," Nate tried to soothe. "Just a little dinner, and we'll be back soon, just me and you. We can call it our practice honeymoon."

She raised her eyebrows. "I'm sorry, but if you're suggesting that he's coming along too—"

Nate offered a smile. "That's not what I meant, and you know it. Look, our honeymoon'll be just you, me, sand, and sea. That's it. Our own little private corner of Heaven. This holiday? Well, we can put up with the excited puppy for a couple of days, surely?"

Charli sighed. She turned to the bed, jumping a little as the pumpkin grinned up at her. "Ew, I forgot that was there." She picked it up gingerly.

It was heavier than she expected. The hard exterior was slick in her hands—almost... sticky—as though the candle's warmth had made its skin sweat. "Gross." She shoved the head into Nate's arms, then turned her attention to the packets of snacks. "Let's get these out of here, too. If I smell any more of this stuff tonight, I'm not going to be able to keep my dinner down."

They worked together to clear the room of all things pumpkin. Nate moved to the doorway, presenting Alex with the pumpkin head as Charli gathered the various packets that crinkled in her arms. When the bed was empty, she moved to the drawers, finding several pumpkin-scented candles which, while unlit, only added to the noxious aroma.

Alex seemed overjoyed at the growing bundle that found its way into his room, Charli starting in alarm as she spotted Alex's own pumpkin sitting on his small walnut desk. He'd propped it on top of a laid-out plaid shirt and chinos, making it seem like a scarecrow had wandered into his room and deflated.

"I'll set this guy up next to him. That way he can have a buddy," Alex said, relishing the discomfort it brought his sister. "Or, Cee-Cee, if you're happy to cut off some of your hair, he can have a girlfriend."

"Freak."

"C'mon," Nate said, stomach rumbling. "Let's get something to eat before everything shuts."

Before they set off, Charli made one last stop to her room. She wandered over to the sash window and, after a little bit of a struggle, managed to raise it a couple inches. A chill autumnal breeze floated its fresh breath into the room. She inhaled deeply, savouring the clean scent of the evening air as the moon shone its silver light upon her. She gave a satisfied nod to the sky, her discomfort easing as the stink began to wash away.

"That's better," she muttered, refusing to let the chatter and chuckling of Nate and Alex waiting in the hall disturb her first quiet moment since entering Brackenholt.

She absently ran her hands on her trousers, wiping away the sticky residue. The lump in her pocket pulled her attention and she took out her phone. Her mood dropped as she stared at the crack on her screen. She thumbed the power button.

The screen stayed black. "Goddamit."

She looked out the window, noticing the view for the first time. Despite her reservations, she couldn't deny that the village was beautiful, like something she'd see in a fairytale. Dozens of homes stretched to her left and right as far as the eye could see. In the distance she spotted a church, the cross standing proud in the night sky as a weathervane gently swung beneath.

Beyond the town borders, rolling hills folded into the horizon, covered in a dense yield of corn. To her immense discomfort, most of the fields were littered with bulbous orange flesh, each vile orb reflecting the moonlight back to her with malicious glee.

Charli stiffened, a small squeak escaping her lips. There, not too far from the darkened frame of a large barn, standing in the middle of one of the pumpkin fields, was a scarecrow.

Its proud pumpkin head stood on top of a supporting crucifix, a flickering light inside its eyes and mouth—an almost direct replica of the pair stationed in their rooms.

"You coming, babe?" Nate asked from the hallway.

Charli shuddered and moved to shut the window. Her imagination ran wild with sudden images of the scarecrow springing to life, sprinting across town, climbing the hotel's walls, and crawling through the window to grab her.

She shook her head, then closed her eyes, allowing herself to remember why she had opened the window in the first place—to let the pumpkin out, not to let the scarecrow in.

She gave a weak laugh.

Nate's voice again, uncertain this time. "Babe?"

"Yeah..." Charli offered softly as she moved away from the window. It was only as she gave a furtive glance back that she noticed something strange.

Where the scarecrow had been looking off to the hills only moments ago, it was now looking directly at Charli.

THREE

Nate and Alex burst into laughter.

Charli let out an exasperated sigh and sat back in the booth. "I swear on my life, it moved."

The bar was small but homely. A large fire roared in the hearth, pumping out a heady heat that made her eyelids heavy. A smattering of locals clinked glasses and chattered as they waited for their food to arrive. Small pumpkins decorated the windows and the bar, each hollowed and carved, grinning at the patrons. Luckily for Charli, the scent of cooked meats, gravy, and potatoes was enough to stifle any whiff of the orange monsters.

"I'm sure it did." Alex scoffed. "And that stag head on the wall just stuck its tongue out at me. Woah! Watch out, it might trot over here and lick us to death." He laughed, then drank a deep measure of his pale ale.

"Forget it," Charli muttered. She hadn't even wanted to bring it up. But there were only so many times Nate could ask her what was wrong before she caved and told her truth.

"Babe, it is a *bit* ridiculous." Nate raised his hands defensively as Charli stared daggers. "What? Can you hear yourself? You're telling us you saw a scarecrow *move*?"

"Listen, I mean... no. I didn't actually *see* it move, but—"

"There you go, then!" Alex's eyes darted around the bar, fixing on a group of young women in the corner. "You're tired. You were overwhelmed by all the pumpkin action in our rooms. It was bound to happen. It's like that time you were convinced that Sir. Bubblington was watching you while you slept."

"That's not fair."

"The bloody fish was dead, Cee-Cee!"

This time Alex was the victim of her stare, though likely through years of suffering his sister's attacks, he'd grown immune.

"Lamb rack?" a voice announced as a shadow fell over their table. The waitress, a middle-aged woman with a tight bob and a tattered apron, held three plates impressively in two hands.

Nate took the lamb. The waitress passed a beef roast to Alex.

"And I'm going to take a stab in the dark and say that the veggie meal is for you, honeybun?"

Charli nodded. The woman slid the plate over, then straightened, hands on her hips. "You guys from out of town?"

"Hmmm?" Alex pulled his attention from the girls in the corner.

"Yes, we are," Nate said with an apologetic look at Alex. "A few counties over. Been driving all day to get here."

"I knew it. I can always tell an out-of-towner just from looks. Here for the picking, I'm guessing?"

Charli frowned. "Yup."

"Oh, don't be so sour, sweetie. It's a hoot. Most gals from outside this place fear getting themselves dirty and messy in the mud. But I tell you, the atmosphere's amazing. Dozens of souls out there in the fields, reaping what we've sown. We get some tunes playing, a few gazebos out front, and we've got ourselves a little festival going. Gonna be especially great this year with that big ol' Harvest Moon, too. Me and Donny go every year, ain't that right, Don?"

She nodded to a disheveled man working behind the bar. The man had a horseshoe of cotton hair, and a sparse beard that looked fit for a teenager bringing in his first bristles. He wiped his forehead with a stained rag, revealing a long, thick bandage that covered his forearm and disappeared into his sleeve. He frowned in their direction. "Wha'sat?"

"The picking!"

"Oh. Yeah. We're blessed, that we are." Donny blinked, then continued his work behind the bar, discomfort sketched in the thick wrinkles on his forehead.

"Is he OK?" Charli asked.

"He's just a lil' slow." The waitress chuckled. "Might just be the reason I married him. Mama always told me you want a man who can limp, not one who can run. You can catch him easier that way. That's the secret to longevity."

Nate and Charli exchanged a look. Luckily, their server missed it.

"Aye, Mama was right and all. Sixteen years married this winter."

"I meant his arm," Charli said. "That's one hell of a bandage."

The waitress leaned against Alex's part of the booth, blinking at her husband with concern. "Hard to say. Came home late the other night. Says he dropped some glass an' caught his forearm. Won't let me see the wound, though. Says it's fine. But I swear he's been acting a little odd since."

"More odd than usual?" Nate asked innocently.

The waitress slapped Nate with her towel. "Hey, that's *my* man. Only I can say things like that. I've earned that right." She offered them all a reassuring smile. "Anyway, best let you get to your eating. Sounds like you've had a long day."

As she sauntered back to the bar, Nate said, "Well, at least we know people around here're friendly."

Alex nodded, his mouth filled with vegetables and potatoes. He swallowed. "Let's hope that extends to the local talent." He glanced to the now empty corner. "Ah, man."

Nate laughed. "Bad luck, amigo. They saw you and managed to escape."

"You're just jealous."

"Of what, exactly?"

As Nate and Alex shot words back and forth like seasoned pros, Charli tuned the pair out. Her fork found her food, found her mouth. Still, her eyes lingered on Donny, stumbling around behind the bar. As he served, he held his injured arm to his chest, barely using his hand to help him. Each customer waited patiently as Donny shambled up and down, a slight drunken lilt to his walk. His forehead glistened with sweat, and no matter how many times he attacked it with his towel, the drops always resurfaced. By the time Charli had finished her food, her intrigue had blossomed into full-grown concern.

"...more pumpkins than Charli can manage."

Charli tuned back in. Alex laughed in her direction.

"Oh, don't tell me you fell asleep with your eyes open again."

Charli frowned, unable to tear her gaze from Donny until he disappeared through a door at the back of the bar.

"No... I..."

"Babe? Everything OK?"

Alex slid his empty plate away, hands patting the mound of his full stomach. "Cee-Cee gets like this sometimes. Just ignore her."

Nate rolled his eyes. "Charli?"

"I'm fine," Charli reassured them both with a weak smile. "Just tired, that's all."

Nate stared at her.

"Honestly, I'm fine. It's just been a long day. A good night's rest will sort everything out, I'm sure."

As the waitress walked past, hands piled high with empty plates, Nate motioned to catch her attention. He asked for the bill and a few moments later she returned.

"Everything OK for you guys?" She flashed a practiced smile, showing patience and calm, betrayed only by the stray lock of hair curling from her head to her cheek.

"Amazing, thank you," Alex replied. "You got a dessert menu?"

Nate flashed him a glare.

"I'm kidding!" Alex shook his head. "Apparently we're *all* full."

The waitress laughed. "Sure you don't want to see desserts? We've got some seasonal specials you might like."

"Let me guess," Charli said. "Pumpkin?"

"You've seen it already?" The waitress winked. "We've got pumpkin pie, pumpkin ice cream, pumpkin crumble, pumpkin cookies, swirls—"

"We get it," Charli cut her off. "Lotta pumpkin."

"That's right." The waitress winked. "I should have saved some of last season's sour grapes for this one."

Behind her, Donny let out a groan of pain, shaking his bandaged arm as though he'd just smacked it against something.

"We just want to pay," Nate told the waitress. "Long day ahead tomorrow. You know how it is."

The waitress seemed to deem this an acceptable excuse, finally handing over the bill.

When they'd settled up, they pulled their coats on, ready to enter the brisk night air. It was as they were leaving, Nate's tall frame having to duck through the tiny door, that Charli looked back over her shoulder to where the waitress had taken over bar duties. Not too far away, Donny sat on an upturned bucket, head hanging, good hand clutching his bandaged arm. Charli wasn't sure if it was a trick of the light, but Donny looked a little off.

Not pale. No. Not even the flushed red of a winter flu.

No.

She could have sworn he looked a little orange.

FOUR

I swear. I saw it. It was there.

I saw it.

Charli lay in bed, covers clutched to her neck in tight fingers. Beside her, Nate slept on, back to her, his bare chest rising and falling with each slow breath. Silver moonlight filtered through the thin curtains, casting shadows that twirled across the walls like spectral ballerinas.

With the windows now closed to keep out the October chill, the smell of putrid pumpkin seeped out of the woodwork, crawled out of the wallpaper, oozed from the cotton bedsheets, turning Charli's stomach and making sleep almost impossible.

I fucking saw it move.

Charli closed her eyes, teeth gritted, recalling her conversation with Nate. Only a brief encounter, but one that triggered her insomnia and kept sleep at bay.

"See, babe? There's nothing there. You must've been imagining things."

Charli had stared out the window, mouth agape. Under the clear night sky, the rolling fields could be seen for miles in all directions. There was the barn, standing as a proud sentinel in the night. She could make out the acne-ridden fields, each pumpkin a pimple on its pubescent face...

But where was the scarecrow?

"No... It was there. I saw it. It was there, I promise."

Nate's hands gently gripped her shoulders. Her hairs stood on end, goosebumps rising at his touch. A gentle breeze licked her exposed flesh.

"You need to sleep," Nate said, soft, slow, soothing in her ear. "Come on. Let's get to bed."

"It was there, Nate. I fucking saw it."

Nate leaned around Charli's side, trying to meet her gaze. "Hey."

Charli remained steadfast.

"Babe..."

His fingers touched her cheek, gently levered her around to face him.

"What?"

"There's no scarecrow." He sighed, frowning. "I'm not sure there ever was."

Her eyes flashed. "You're saying I'm lying?"

He motioned to the window. "Where is it? Scarecrows don't just get up and wander off. If it was there earlier, it would be there now." He ran a hand through his hair. Usually, the untidy ruffle made her pulse quicken, but tonight Charli couldn't focus. "Look, I'm not saying that... I'm just... Look, it's been a long day. A lot's happened. Maybe your mind was playing tricks on you because of the, erm, unique welcome the hotel set out for us."

Charli dropped her gaze to the windowsill. Her hands were clenched into fists at her side.

Nate stroked her arm. He gently encouraged her toward

the bed, closing the window behind him. "C'mon, babe. A good night's sleep is just what the doctor ordered."

Charli joined him, failing to quell the rising irritation as Nate fell asleep in minutes. Despite his assurances of a good rest, Charli seethed. Heat flushed her chest. Irritation flared her nostrils. It wouldn't have been so bad were it not for that sickly odour choking the air. How could she possibly have made it all up? She had seen it with her own two eyes. It had been there in the middle of the fucking field. One minute it had been looking away, the next it had been staring straight at her with flaming eyes.

Why would there be a lit candle in an outdoor scarecrow?

She glared at Nate, more irritated by his kindness than by his refusal to believe her. Arguing was easier when there was some anger in it. But the way he had looked at her...

Maybe I am *tired,* Charli mused, not convinced in her own thoughts.

She stared at the ceiling, watching the shapes that folded and coalesced above. Outside, the world whispered in darkness, the occasional chirp of a cricket or the hoot of an owl the only sounds in an otherwise sedate world.

Charli wasn't sure how long she had lain there, rest a distant thing, when she heard the rustling.

She rose slowly, not wanting to disturb Nate. Though he was sympathetic to Charli's occasional bouts of insomnia, he suffered if he didn't get his eight hours of beauty sleep. She crept to the window, fingers finding the cold sill. Her first instinct was to stare out into the fields.

Nothing. Empty.

Charli pinched her nose.

Stupid.

Moaning from the street below.

There. Movement.

Someone stumbled around the corner, almost falling as they staggered into the center of the road. Under the soft buttery glow of the lamplight Charli couldn't make out a face. Only the shambling silhouette.

She pressed her hand to the glass, close enough for her breath to mist the surface.

The man was shirtless. He wore loose-fitting pajama pants that ruffled in the breeze. Hunched over, one hand clawed at the opposite forearm as he incessantly scratched at the skin. He looked like he was under the influence of... something... swaying about the space as he walked on without aim.

Charli leaned even closer. Nose touching the glass. She barely breathed as the man walked beneath the lamppost outside the hotel. He tripped, scraped his stomach and let out a pain-filled growl. Something slick stained the ground.

Charli gasped.

The man looked up, dark eyes locking onto hers.

A single word escaped Charli's lips. "Donny..."

Another voice. "There you are!"

Charli watched on in silence as the waitress from the bar ran across the street, her bare feet silent on the brick. A blanket flapped behind her as she ran, and as she met her husband, she threw it over his shoulders.

Charli didn't blink. Couldn't look away from this absurd theater.

"This way, honey," the waitress coaxed, addressing him the way a mother would encourage a child, yet with an edge to her voice that betrayed her concern. She looked around, ensuring that no one was watching as she guided Donny back the way he'd come. He resisted to begin with, then relented, head falling onto her shoulder.

All too soon, they vanished.

Silence.

Charli finally blinked, suddenly aware that at some point her mouth had fallen open. She replayed the scene in her head, already doubting Nate and Alex would believe her when she told them what she'd seen.

She was sure about one thing, though.

Something was wrong with Donny. The dark patch still stained the moonlit street. And that scratching... had that been the same arm that Donny had been fighting to keep covered?

Something wasn't right. But what logical explanation could she give to what she had just seen?

Somewhere in the back of her mind, an absurd thought was beginning to take root. An impossible thought that could only be the result of hunger, dehydration, and exhaustion from a long trip.

Or so she forced herself to believe.

CHAPTER

FIVE

C harli could count on one hand the number of hours she slept that night.

She'd watched the bedside clock, waiting for its shrill call to welcome the morning. When it finally did, she waited a moment for Nate to rouse, then turned off the alarm.

"Morning, babe."

"Hi," she replied, flat.

Nate stretched. Usually, Charli loved seeing Nate in the mornings. It was one of her favorite times of the day, when his hair was askew and he had that lazy glow about him.

But not today.

"How did you sleep?" Nate asked.

"Like a baby."

The lie tasted sour as soon as it escaped her lips, but after replaying the strange events of last night in her head a thousand times, she'd already convinced herself that Nate wouldn't believe her. Again.

She wasn't sure she believed herself.

I saw the barman. Donny. He was in the street last night.

29

Charli...

He's not well. Bled all over the floor. The waitress had to take him home.

Yeah, right.

It just wasn't worth it. She didn't want to start their first full day in Brackenholt in a sour mood. Though, as she rose from bed and started getting dressed, she paused at the window, an involuntary yelp coming from her lips.

The scarecrow was back.

"Everything OK?" Nate asked. "You seem a little down. You're going to have to work that energy up for today. Lots of picking to be done."

Charli started to reply, wanting to tell Nate that the straw freakshow was there, but before she could, a rap sounded on their door.

"Morning lovebirds! Rise and shine!"

Charli rolled her eyes at the sound of Alex's voice. Nate cast her an apologetic look.

"I'm loving our romantic getaway," Charli said softly.

Nate stood and wrapped his arms around her. He was still shirtless, and despite everything, Charli fell into him.

"He's just excited," Nate whispered.

"But..."

The knocking got louder. "Hey! You guys up? I heard movement."

Charli stepped back from Nate's arms and pointed to the door. "Well, go on then. Better go let the puppy out before he wets himself."

Alex's mouth was full when Nate opened the door. He beamed. One of his hands was lost in a brightly colored bag of pumpkin seeds.

"Could you just... not... please?" Charli said, turning her attention to straightening the bed. Although she assumed the hotel would have a room cleaner, she could never shake the lessons instilled in her from an early age.

Tidy room, tidy mind.

"You sound like Mom." Alex clutched a handful of seeds and held them out to Nate. "Mate, have you tried these? They're ridiculously addictive. Dunno if it's the salt or whatever, but I can't get enough."

"Not the biggest fan of seeds," Nate said.

"Oh, go on," Alex pushed. "Live a little. We're in a new place. Trying new things. They're not going to bite you. Here."

Nate considered the offering. He relented, plucking two from the pile before throwing them into his mouth.

"Not bad," Nate admitted. "Not sure they're going to become my go-to snack, but not bad at all. I still prefer pie though."

"I've got bags of these things in my room," Alex said. "Not sure who's in charge of the minibar, but it seems that every time I finish a bag, there's another waiting." He licked at the stains off the end of his fingers, frowning slightly when an orange hue persisted on his skin.

"And you're sure they don't charge you for those?" Nate said. "Aren't minibars normally quite pricey?"

Alex shrugged, his mouth already full of another handful.

Charli joined in. "If they do charge, Alex is paying."

Alex held up his hands in surrender. "Fine. Fine. Jesus. I'm only trying to spread the local joy. I'm loving little village life." He swallowed loudly, tongue playing over the pieces of seed stuck in his teeth. "Speaking of which, these seeds are only making me hungrier. Breakfast?"

The morning was bright when they all stepped outside, the sun lying low against the horizon. Despite its intensity, the sun's warmth did nothing to combat the air's chill.

They found a small corner shop and grabbed something to go. Charli struggled to find something that wasn't in some way spiced by pumpkin extract or which contained the fruit, settling instead for a selection of garden variety apples. As they made their way toward the fields, Charli remained quiet, letting Nate and Alex talk excitedly about their day ahead, her gaze occasionally drifting, searching for the scarecrow. With each step she questioned her life choices. How had a suggestion for a romantic weekend turned into a three-day escape to a backwater pumpkin-obsessed town? It was all beyond her.

Especially when her mind appeared to be playing tricks on her. Or perhaps a sentient scarecrow was actually breaking free of his cross and stalking through the town at night.

This is why you don't let your brother suggest ideas to you and his best mate when you're drunk. You wake up in the morning and... Bam! Non-refundable tickets and a weekend in the mud.

Her hand reached instinctively for the phone in her pocket. She let out an audible sigh when it came up empty.

"Charli? You OK?" Nate's voice came from far away.

As Charli squinted through the bright sunshine, noting the barn a mile or so ahead, she offered a weak smile. "Yeah. Fine. Just a little tired."

Signs littered the way as they drew closer to their destination, hand-drawn and childlike. In Charli's opinion, the worst was a sketch of a bright orange pumpkin with a beaming face. Soon, the pathways grew busy with foot traffic as locals converged.

At first, it was small clusters of two or three people, but

by the time Charli was close enough to read the words [Farmer Jack's Pumpkin Patch] scrawled across the top of the open barn doors, there were close to one hundred volunteers milling around.

They fell in line behind a throng of locals. Charli couldn't believe it. There were people of all ages and genders. Mothers with bright-eyed children in tiny overalls and boots. Elderly couples with silver hair glowing white in the sunlight, and toothish grins on their faces. There were younger couples and groups of friends, and even a few solo stragglers, content in their own company. Before long, a voice called out over the crowd.

At first, Charli couldn't hear him properly. But as they worked their way closer and into the shade of the musty barn, they found a plump, rosy-cheeked man standing on a bale of hay with a clipboard in hand.

"Keep coming! Keep coming! Move forward! Closer, now! Speak to one of our advisors just over here and we'll assign your quarter. Don't worry, there's room for everyone! The more the merrier!"

Nate reached for Charli's hand. Alex's neck worked on a swivel, trying to eye up the local talent. There was a strangeness to his eyes, as though their color had changed slightly, but before Charli could take a closer look, they were shepherded toward two frazzled women wearing yellow and orange hi-vis jackets.

Charli, Alex, and Nate were assigned a quarter of a nearby field, and each given a pair gardening gloves, as well as a set of thick, curved pruning shears. Only a few moments later they were back in the bright sunshine, hands shading their brows as they searched for 'B4'.

"It's like battleships," Alex said, staring out over the rolling countryside. Despite the hour, workers were already busying themselves with pruning pumpkins from the vine and placing them in the large wooden crates stationed about the field.

"But definitely not as fun," Charli said, her nose wrinkling at the raw scent of damp earth and thick green leaves. She was a long way from the familiar smells of inner-city life.

"You guys lost?"

They all turned in the direction of the perky voice, a slight country twang to the woman's words.

Alex was the first to acknowledge her, shocking neither Charli nor Nate. She must've been in her late teens, and wore her hair in long pigtails, complete with a wide-brimmed sun hat. Blue overalls covered her body, and despite the sun, she wore a thick, long-sleeved undershirt that covered most of her skin. She had a smattering of freckles across her cheeks and a slight cleft in her chin.

"Well, we're not exactly lost, but you can show us where to go," Alex said, a goofy smile plastered on his flushed face. Nate and Charli chuckled.

"It's a lot to take in, the first pick," the woman said. "Especially for out-of-towners." She offered a hand to Alex. "Stacey."

"Alex." Alex eagerly accepted her hand, unable to take his eyes off her. "Nice to meet you. This is my buddy, Nate, and my sister, Charli."

More hand shaking, more wide smiles—for the boys, at least. Charli made to offer her own hand in greeting, but Stacey, whose attention had been fixed on Nate, tucked hers into a large pocket on the front of her overalls instead. "Where're you guys stationed?"

"B4," Alex said.

"Oh, yay. Same as us." Stacey beamed as two women

strode up behind her. "This is Esther and Harley. Girls, it's time to show the new blood the ropes."

Harley and Esther offered hands to Alex who greedily accepted. When Nate took a step forward, Charli pulled him back, hooking her arm in his. Harley and Esther made no effort to greet them.

"B4's at the back," Stacey said. "Come on. This way."

Alex took pride of place next to Stacey as he engaged her in conversation. Nate and Charli walked several steps behind, though Charli could sense Nate's attention drifting forward. When they arrived at a cordoned square of the patch, the women led them to a large and battered wooden crate, easily the length of Alex's car, ready and waiting for that morning's produce deposits.

"Cut the vines, pick the pumpkins, and place them gently in here," Stacy said.

"Easy enough," Alex replied with a grin. "Chop, pick, and chuck."

"*Gently*," Harley emphasized, her grin withering.

"We don't damage the pumpkins," Esther added.

Harley's eyes hardened. "Ever."

Alex raised placating hands. "OK. Gently. Got it."

The smile returned instantly to Harley's face.

Charli looked around their square. Trailing across the loamy soil was a bed of green vines blossoming with bright orange pumpkins. The hotel clerk was right—she'd never seen them so large. The ones she'd seen at supermarkets had only ever been about a foot tall. Farmer Jack's pumpkins grew up to her thighs and were so round and swollen that she already knew she wouldn't be able to fit her arms around them.

She turned to Nate, making sure they were out of

earshot of the others, "How the hell am I supposed to pick these things up?"

Nate grinned. "We'll have to work as a team. Roll them? Would be a nice bonding exercise."

"They're not as heavy as they look," Stacey said.

Charli shot her a look that instantly said, 'Mind your own business, bitch.'

"Us country girls have no problem picking these. The bigger, the better, right, ladies?" She laughed. Harley and Esther giggled.

Harley even flexed a toned bicep.

"Still, we can split into pairs, can't we?" Alex asked eagerly. "I'm a city boy, too. Might need a helping hand to get me going."

"Oh, no, handsome, you're with me." Stacey winked, then turned on her heels, striding to the far corner with Alex in tow. Harley and Esther went off in another direction.

Charli watched her brother for a moment, concern etched on her brow. It wasn't unusual for him to thirst after female attention, but something plucked at the hairs on the back of Charli's neck.

"You ready to go, pumpkin?" Nate asked, laughing at his own joke.

"Don't..."

Nate stood beside Charli, tracking her line of vision. "It's a good thing he's made a friend. Means we get some more of that time together that you wanted, eh? Me and you. Stacey can distract the tagalong."

"Mmm..."

"What is it?" There was a hint of exasperation on Nate's face that he failed to hide.

"It's just... don't you find them a little... odd?" Charli asked.

"Odd how?"

"Just... a little weird."

Nate ran his fingers through his hair. "No weirder than I'd expect. This kind of life's different to the one we're used to. Of course we're going to find them a little... unusual." An older man walked past the pair, gently easing his pumpkin into the crate. He flashed his eyes to Nate. "Sorry, sir. Not you. I mean, no offense, I'm sure you're—"

The man rolled his eyes and walked away.

Nate marveled. "Did he just pick that up by himself?"

"Nate..." Charlie started.

"Babe." Nate's brows set. "We're here now. We're in the middle of the field that we traveled miles to get to. Let's just try to make the best of it, yeah? Me and you. Who knows? You might just enjoy yourself." Nate snipped his shears in the air a couple of times, eyebrows wriggling.

Charli laughed, the weight that had been sinking on her chest lightening just a touch. "OK, lover boy. Show me what you've got."

Charli drew her own shears from her pocket as Nate bent down to clip his first vine. Bodies busily moved about them as the harvest began. She heard Alex laughing with Stacey, already smitten by the stranger.

And then, there it was. Far off to their right, standing in the center of the adjacent field, a sight that made her smile vanish: a single crucifix made from reconstituted wood that bore the oversized body of the scarecrow.

SIX

From where Charli stood, she could only make out the back of its head—bulbous and orange and offensive.

She had never understood scarecrows. How could a static figure scare off murders of crows and hungry gulls from pecking at the farmer's seed? It seemed a ridiculous notion. Like, couldn't the birds just work out that the scarecrow was never going to come alive and chase them away? Weren't crows supposed to be smart?

But now, as she stared across the field, she began to understand. Even from this distance, she felt its aura. The body of the scarecrow was pretty damned realistic beneath its hessian clothing. Despite the fact its legs didn't quite touch the ground, Farmer Jack had done a great job of twisting and manipulating the straw to resemble a human body. The head might have been a little too swollen to be truly convincing, but overall, it wasn't half bad.

"There. First one done. A gazillion more to go." Nate proudly rolled a large pumpkin toward Charli's feet. "Everything OK?"

"Yeah," Charli replied. "All good."

Despite the ominous totem in the fields, she forced herself to engage. She was shocked by the weight of the first pumpkin as they worked together to hook their arms beneath the orange orb and lift it into the crate. On their first few attempts their hands slipped, and on another, Charli got too excited and hoisted too soon, causing the pumpkin to roll free from their grasp and onto the ground.

"*Gently,*" Charli said, mimicking Harley's instructions.

Nate snorted.

Finally, they found their rhythm. They deliberately stayed close enough to the crate that they didn't have to walk too far, but Charli was impressed to see that, despite having only been there a few minutes, half a dozen pumpkins already filled the lower section of the container.

"Impressive, ain't it?" A stout woman with arms like tree trunks winked as she placed her own pumpkin down. "You'll be surprised how quickly these fill up. Some volunteers make several trips back and forth emptying and providing new crates." She nodded to the barn. "You'll hear the whistle soon enough. When that sounds, you stop. It's the only water break we get."

Charli's eyebrows raised. The woman roared with laughter and returned to her patch before Charli or Nate could respond.

The morning passed quickly—much to Charli's delight. Although it only took an hour for her body to start aching, she managed to keep pace with Nate. Working together, alongside the others, their crate was soon filled, and just as it looked as if it might overflow, a shrill whistle shrieked across the fields.

All field hands stood up. Some volunteers remained where they were, waiting for their new crate to arrive.

Others wandered toward the barn to catch a few moments of reprieve in the shade. Others unshouldered backpacks and took out bottles to quench their thirst.

"Shit." Nate muttered as the gentle rumble of a forklift rolled toward them. "We should've thought ahead. I assumed they'd provide refreshments."

"They do." A lanky man stood beside them, hands on hips. He had a wispy beard that drifted in the wind and an angular, beak-like nose. "Inside the barn. Jack's usually pretty good about that. Sets up some water. A few snacks. Not enough to feed an army, but just enough for all of us."

Charli smiled, recognising the man who had been picking only a short distance from the pair all morning.

"I can show you where to go if you like?"

Nate looked at Charli, his eyebrow arched.

Charli nodded. "Thanks. That would be lovely."

As they made their way to the barn, Charli openly stared at the crowd. Only a short distance ahead she spotted the burly woman with thick arms, laughing with two children that couldn't have been much older than eight and ten. Not too far away from them, a group of teenage boys jostled and guffawed loudly. Just in front of them were several silver-haired men and women with hunched backs and slow strides.

"It really is a communal event," the lanky man offered, following Charli's gaze.

"Looks that way," Charli replied. "We don't get much of this at home. In the city, people are everywhere, but you never truly feel connected."

"That's sad." The old man's smile slipped. He scratched absently at his neck, then let out a chesty cough into the ring of his fist. "Well, hopefully you don't feel that way here. I'm Terrence."

He offered the hand he had just coughed in. Charli looked warily at the thin skin, knobbly bones and fingers.

She faltered. Terrence's fingertips were orange.

After an uncomfortable pause, Nate intercepted, accepting the man's hand. "Nice to meet you, Terrence."

"Pleasure's all mine. Y'all let me know if you need anything, OK? This is a team effort. There's no 'I' in 'pumpkin picking.'"

Before Charli or Nate could correct Terrence's backwards wisdom, he chuckled, waved to someone he knew, and strode off ahead.

"He's not wrong," Nate said cheerily.

"You're kidding, right?"

Nate laughed. "There isn't *an* 'I.' There're three."

Charli scoffed.

They closed in on the barn. Bodies bustled, packed tightly inside the building. Most field hands stood with a cup in their hands, while others wove their way through the throng to several long tables.

As Charli battled her way through with Nate, her nose wrinkled. The sweetly noxious tang from her room had returned.

She shuddered. While the smell hadn't bothered her out on the fields, it now closed in on her, stronger than the residue of livestock barn stink that festered in the gathered bales of hay in the corners.

And one quick look ahead revealed its source. It was all that the crowd were consuming. Bright foil packets clutched in fists. Pumpkin seeds and bakes and even sticky orange sweets for the little ones.

In one corner, a table was set up with an orange gingham cloth. Four permed and wrinkled ladies proudly displayed their homemade wares, gratefully offered in exchange for donations to the local Homemaker's Association, speaking through false-toothed grins, sticky with fruit pulp.

When Charli and Nate finally made it to the free refreshments, Charli's mood worsened.

She glared at the overflowing bowls. "Absolutely not."

Even the large, sweating glass containers at the drinks station were filled with pumpkin juice. A smaller dispenser sat nearby, barely a finger of water left at the bottom.

Nate's arm wrapped around Charli's shoulder, already detecting her disgust. "I guess it makes sense. They want to celebrate the very things we're picking." He kissed her temple. "I'm sorry, I know this isn't ideal for you."

"They couldn't even put out coffee?"

"You sure you don't want to *try* some? Who knows, you might like it. When was the last time you—"

Bile rose in Charli's throat as the smell of porcelain and bleach flooded her nostrils. An acidic bubble popped in her stomach as the memory of half-chewed orange goo expelling between clamped teeth flashed in her mind.

She closed her eyes, taking a deep breath. "I'll be fine. Don't worry about it."

She helped herself to the meagre drop of water. Meanwhile, Nate piled his plate high with the remaining food. Just as Charli drew alongside Nate and was about to take a sip, someone crashed into the side of her.

What little there was of Charli's water spilled over her trousers and onto the barn floor. She grunted, mind flashing with two pumpkin-headed children and a cracked phone. "Fucks sake, watch where you're going!"

Stacey's smile stretched from ear to ear as she regained her balance. Small flecks of pulp peeked from between her teeth.

"Oops," she said, satisfied sarcasm edging her words.

"What did you do that for?"

"Oh, don't be silly. It's this uneven floor." Stacey winked, then leaned toward Nate, her top button popping open. "I've never met a girl with so little meat on her bones. You might want to re-think your options, darling. The gals in this town can show you what it's like to be with a real woman."

Rage churned in Charli's stomach. "Excuse me?"

Nate stepped between them. "Come on, babe. She's not worth it."

Alex appeared beside them, his mouth full of orange mush, oblivious to what had just happened. "Hey! There you are! I've been looking for you. Lush spread, huh?"

Stacey's eyes bore into Charli's. "Not for this one, apparently. She's too good for our harvest."

"Seriously, what is your problem?" Charli's nails dug into her palms, but all she wanted to do was tear them along Stacey's plump cheeks and wipe that smirk right off her face.

"No problem here." Stacey shrugged. "Since there's nothing else left, I guess you'll just have to quench that thirst on our homegrown produce, won't you? It won't be so bad. Your boyfriend is clearly happy to experiment and try something new."

Charli growled. "*Fiancé.*"

She shouldn't have bothered. Stacey had already hooked her arm around Alex and was leading the shambling fool away.

"Is there any point asking if you're OK?" Nate looked sheepish as he searched Charli's face.

"No. There isn't. What the hell was that all about? What did I ever do to that bitch?"

"I guess not everyone takes kindly to out-of-towners," Nate offered. "Let's just keep away from her from now on. Let Alex keep her distracted until we leave. We can still make the most of this, babe."

Still fuming, Charli searched the crowd for Stacey and Alex.

They were gone.

Not a trace.

Not too far away, Esther and Harley stood and watched them, unblinking, their cups full to the brims with clear water.

Nate looked down at Charli with pity. He offered his cup of pumpkin juice. "Last time I ask. Promise. Did you want to give it a go?"

Charli didn't take her eyes off the girls. "No. I'd rather go thirsty than drink that shit."

Nate followed Charli's gaze, but the girls were gone. "You need to keep up your strength. We've still got a whole afternoon to go."

Charli clenched her jaw, her eyes catching on a flash of blue overalls and a straw hat. "It's fine. I'll just see if Jack has more water in the back or something."

She left Nate behind, determined to find a way to slake her thirst. The crowd was thick, volunteers reluctant to allow her through. All around her they greedily shoved their free snacks into their mouths. Most were chatting animatedly, but Charli couldn't help but notice a few members of the throng staring vacantly into space, their lips stained as they swayed gently on the spot.

"Excuse me!" Charli called, catching up with the man who had been giving orders earlier—the one she assumed was Farmer Jack. "Excuse me!"

The man was middle-aged, with a red plaid shirt

stretched over his sizable paunch. Despite the cloying heat of the body-filled barn, he wore long sleeves beneath his overalls and sported dark sweat patches beneath his armpits. He wore thick picking gloves and Charli wondered why he still had them on.

"You're Farmer Jack, right?" Charli asked.

"Huh?" the man replied, eyeing Charli curiously.

"The guy who owns this place. It's Farmer Jack's Pumpkin Patch? Says it right there on your shirt."

The man let out a raucous laugh, drawing the gaze of several volunteers. "Oh, my. No, you're mistaken, I'm not Jack. My name's Stephen, or Farmer Stephen, depending on your persuasion."

"Oh." Charli frowned. "So, you don't own the farm?"

"I do." Stephen grinned and winked. Beneath the thick bristles of brown beard Charli spotted several missing teeth. One of his eyes was slightly clouded. "It's my farm. But I don't go by Jack."

"Then why is it called 'Farmer Jack's'?"

The broad man gave a crooked grin and nodded toward the barn doors. "That'll be 'cause of our mascot. Jack. S'what we call that dear old fella watching our crops."

Charli followed where Stephen was pointing. "The scarecrow?"

"Aye, though don't call him that. He doesn't like that."

"What, 'scarecrow'?"

Stephen put a finger to his lips conspiratorially. "He's much more than that, dear. He's a protector. A guardian. Keeps us blessed, he does. There's an uncanny magic in that straw fella."

Charli's eyes widened. "Magic?"

"Oh, aye. Comes alive, he does. Walks the fields. Flaps away the birds and keeps them at bay. Has done for decades. He's much, much more than *just* a scarecrow. He's our main man, is Jack."

Charli let out a slow breath. "I knew it."

"Did you now?" Stephen said softly.

"The scarecrow... I knew it. He's real? I mean... *alive*?"

He met her gaze for a long moment, head tilted to one side. Something strange flickered in his eyes. Then, without warning, he let out a brassy laugh, hands clutching his stomach. "Oh, my! You lot are a gullible sort, aren't you?"

Charli frowned. "But you said..."

"Of course he's not real!" Stephen wiped a tear from his eye. A couple of heads turned their way. "He's a fruit ball stuck on a stack of straw with one of my old coats. I picked him fresh myself only a few days ago. What did you think he was? Not been listening to Miss Turnberry's old wives' tales, have ya?"

"No... it's just..." Embarrassment colored Charli's cheeks. "Forget it."

"Oh, my!" Stephen's laughter died, and pity took its place. "Urban myths aside, did you need something? I'm presuming you didn't find me just so I can regale some idle legends?"

Charli bit back her preferred response, instead asking if there was any more water.

"'fraid not. That's all I've got without running all the way back to the farm. Plenty of juice to go around though, packed with nutrients and other goodies. We're a lucky bunch. Been a plentiful crop this year. It's like poetry, ain't it? Harvest moon on a harvest night on Halloween, of all nights. Come tomorrow night, there'll be pumpkins on the ground, and one big one high up in the sky." Farmer Stephen lifted a drink to his lips, the clear water splashing gently against his bristled lips.

"So, we've been told," Charli said, frowning as her gaze fixed on the drink.

Stephen took another sip. "Anything else?"

Charli shook her head, unable to shake off the strange feeling that the farmer was rubbing his drink choice in her face. "Look, I'm sorry to have bothered you."

"Not at all." As Charli stepped away, Stephen called after her. "And watch out for Jack! Remember, don't call him a scarecrow, or he'll have something to say about it!"

Charli slunk off in search of Nate. At first, she couldn't find him anywhere, but as the volunteers drifted through the doors back toward the fields and the crowds thinned, she spotted him near the barnyard doors...

...deep in conversation with Stacey, Alex standing nearby with a vacant grin on his face.

Heat rose inside Charli, vivid, pulsing, burning. She swallowed dryly, internally prepping herself for a long afternoon ahead.

SEVEN

C harli worked in silence.

The afternoon grew warm, the last vestiges of light from the setting sun casting a pale glow among the workers. Sweat poured down Charli's neck, draining her of fluids she couldn't afford to replace. Her throat was dry and sore. As the day wore on, her mood dropped, and her head spun with each pumpkin she and Nate chopped from the vine and piled into the crate.

Nate had tried to talk to Charli. But she knew his heart wasn't in it. As they'd walked back to their patch after their break, Stacey had skipped ahead with Alex trailing along behind her. Though Nate tried to hide it from his face, Charli saw the merest hint of resentment flicker across his face. He'd asked if she was OK. Charli had given a simple 'No,' then walked off with pressed lips and a bubbling irritation. Nate had been all too happy talking to a woman who, only moments before, had purposefully bashed into her and spilled the only drink she'd had access to.

Charli wasn't about to give Stacey that satisfaction.

And now, here they were, stooped over in backbreaking

silence. Charli's fingertips burned. Her thighs ached. Dry mud caked her brand-new walking boots, and she was sweating from places she didn't know she could sweat from.

She stood, wiping a thick sheen of perspiration from her forehead. She watched Alex following Stacey like a shadow. He parroted her every step. Each sentence that left her ripe lips had him chuckling like a love-drunk teen.

"Hey, check it out."

Nate laid on the ground, a pumpkin wedged beneath the stretched fabric of his shirt, making him appear robustly pregnant. Above his belt, a wide smile of orange gave the pumpkin away. "You always wanted kids, didn't you? Meet our firstborn." He grinned stupidly, eyes hopeful for a laugh. "We can call him Todd, after your dad."

Charli blinked once.

Twice.

She bent down to work at the next vine. Anger boiled inside her, threatening to spill. She kept her mouth shut because she knew it wasn't completely rational. Dehydration and hunger affected her mood, and it wouldn't be fair to take it out on Nate. But, by all that was holy, she wanted to. With each tinkle of Stacey's laughter that floated across the wind, her jaw clenched tighter. With each stupid joke that Nate made to try and break her mood, Charli only grew more steadfast in her frustration.

Not too long after, Nate gave up.

By the time the sun reached the horizon and the blue sky turned mauve and orange, Charli was near breaking point. She put both hands on her hips and exhaled as the whistle blew for the end of the day. Her body screamed for a bath. Her mind longed for food, drink, and sleep.

"That's one day done," Nate said dryly, not looking at Charli. "One more to go."

"Thank God for that."

Charli headed for the barn without waiting for Nate. All she could focus on was collapsing in bed and sleeping off the last horrid twenty-four hours. The weekend couldn't pass quickly enough.

Nate tried to take her hand, but she pulled away. He huffed, and matched her pace, their bodies close, their minds worlds apart.

"Hey, slow down!" Alex appeared beside them. "This is great stuff, right? I never knew how much I'd enjoy getting my hands dirty and working the land."

Nate side-eyed his friend. "You mean how much you'd enjoy spending your day with a cute out-of-towner who clearly has the hots for you?"

Charli glared at Nate.

He rolled his eyes and exhaled slowly. "Babe, I'm not saying *I* think she's cute. It's just..."

"Forget it," Alex interjected. "She's clearly fed up. You're going to get nothing out of her right now. We call this her 'hangry' phase. Right, Cee-Cee?"

Charli's nostrils flared.

"Point and case," Alex said. "Still, the girls were saying they're heading to The Copper Bell for some food and drinks tonight. They want to know if we'll join them."

Charli scoffed. "That bar we went to last night?"

"Might be nice," Nate said.

Charli stopped in her tracks. "You promised we'd have some alone time together." She searched Nate's eyes, wondering if she was going mad from the heat and lack of sleep, or if the usual twinkle in his bright eyes was missing today.

"And we will," Nate replied. "But we're going to need to get some food first anyway, and the only thing we've got in the hotel is pumpkin."

"Thanks for reminding me!" Alex clapped his hands, then fished some seeds from his pocket. "Mmm, sooo good!"

"Will you fuck off for a minute?" Charli barked.

Alex held up his hands. "Wow. Fine. I'll go find Stace. Tell her at least one of us is up for some fun." He winked, then humped the air before running ahead to where Stacey was waiting for him by the barn doors.

"Babe..." Nate began.

"Don't fucking 'babe' me, Nate. This isn't OK. First, you promise me that we'll spend some time together tonight... *alone*. Now? Oh, surprise, surprise, you've changed your mind, and you want to go out with *them*. And, for some fucked up reason, the only food I'm able to get my hands on in this backwater shithole is disgusting, and the only chance for a decent drink I had today was knocked out of my hands by a rural bimbo. Who, incidentally, has somehow glamored my brother into acting like a horny schoolboy. I'm telling you, something's not *fucking* right."

Nate pinched the bridge of his nose, and in that moment, Charli hated herself, seeing how much her behavior was affecting him.

"Babe... are you sure this isn't still to do with the—"

"Oh, hell no. You don't get to bring up that shitting scarecrow!" Charli took a step back, gaze snapping to the sentinel guard standing lonely in the vacated field. "That's not what this is about. Christ Almighty, I just want to spend some of the time I was promised with my supposed partner."

"And we will." Nate stepped toward her. "Let's just get

some food and drink first. You're starving. You're thirsty. You've been working all day. It's putting you in a—"

"Be very fucking careful with the next words that come out of your—"

"—mood. We'll get a good meal, then head up to the hotel. Leave Alex with his groupies for the night. I'm sure that's what he really wants anyway."

Charli looked to the barn, expecting Alex to be waiting for them. There was no sign of him, or the three Bitches of Brackenholt.

"Promise?" Charli asked.

"Promise."

Nate smiled, but as Charli met his eyes, she couldn't shake the feeling that something was off. "We need to clean up first, though."

"OK." Charli fell into his arms. "A hot shower, a decent meal, and one, very, very strong drink."

CHAPTER

EIGHT

Charli was the first to shower, lathering up an unholy amount of soap to remove the day's toil. When her skin was pink, she set about drying her hair while Nate attended to his own hygiene. As Charli sat in the chair at the small walnut desk, she found herself already feeling a little better. As if all she needed was a good cooldown to wash away the grime that had made its way beneath her skin.

Nate stepped out of the shower looking like the god she had fallen in love with. A plain white towel wrapped around his waist, his body glistened, all toned muscles and fine hair, made only more appealing by the day's labor. She digested him with a look and bit her lip.

Nate's eyebrow arched. "Now?"

Charli looked past Nate to the door. "I don't know. Think my baby brother will give us long enough to finish?"

His glorious smile widened. "What do you think? And I thought *you* were the baby."

"You've killed the mood, babe. Anyway, he's only older

by a minute," Charli said, deciding her next move in her head.

Alex's voice came through the walls, his enthusiastic singing muffled.

"Ew. Yeah, it's gone. Maybe later," Charli said.

Nate shrugged, then set about drying himself and getting dressed.

Once they were both ready, Charli drifted over to the window. Jack was out there, standing tall against his cross. She could make out his slight silhouette beneath the pale light of the moon. Nate padded up behind Charli and wrapped his arms around her. "Is he still there?"

A shadow flickered across Charli's face. She couldn't tell whether he was mocking or being sincere. "Yup." Her stomach rumbled painfully.

She peeled herself from Nate's embrace and stepped into the hallway, thoughts consumed by food. She knocked on her brother's hotel door.

Inside, silence.

"What is it?" Nate asked, locking the door behind them.

The hallway was quiet. Another knock on the door. She pressed her ear to the wood. Still no reply. "He's gone."

A crunching came from behind Charli. She turned to find Nate cocking an eyebrow, mouth full of pumpkin seeds.

"Huh? Oh. Well, I'm sure he'll be OK."

Charli shuddered. She wasn't so sure.

CHAPTER
NINE

Charli darted through the old bar door, Nate close on her heels.

The cloying heat from the bar wafted over her. Her hair stuck flat to her head, shoulders damp from the sudden onslaught of rain that had opened from the heavens the moment they exited the hotel. Though Charli had wanted a cab, Nate insisted the journey would be short and the rain would soon pass.

It had not.

She shook off the worst of the downpour and scanned the packed room. Compared to the previous night, the place was heaving, with a line three people deep gathered around the bar. Tables were bustling with patrons, and an uncomfortably familiar sweet smell filled the air.

"Maybe we should find somewhere else."

"There he is." Nate pointed over to the far corner of the room. Alex stood beside a chair, animatedly in discussion with Stacey, Esther, Harley, and a few unfamiliar faces. "Told you we'd find him."

"Wonder what's gotten into him," Charli mused.

"I think it's more what's trying to get *onto* him," Nate said, the wingman in him coming out with a smirk. "Maybe tonight will be the night. Look at the way she's groping him."

Stacey's hand stroked up and down Alex's arm, a lustful hunger gleaming in her eyes.

They made their way through the throng to the table. At first, Alex didn't even notice them, but when Nate cleared his throat and tapped his shoulder, he offered them a warm welcome.

"Hey buddy! I wondered when you two were gonna show up."

"You said you were going to wait for us." Charli scanned for a spare chair and found none.

Alex waved a hand. His cheeks were rosy, forehead beaded with perspiration. He had clearly already eaten, judging by the empty plate in front of him. "Ah, come on. You think I'm going to waste my time waiting for you guys while you get your freak on?"

"Alex..." Nate attempted.

"Oh! I'm sorry, I totally forgot. It wouldn't be that long of a wait." He pointed a thumb at Nate as he addressed the table. "Cee-Cee's a lucky woman, getting hitched to Captain One-Pump-and-Dump."

To Charli's surprise, Nate grabbed Alex's shoulder and pulled him closer, whispering in his ear. The mirth dropped from Alex's face. Charli noted that her brother's pupils looked wholly dilated, his eyes holding no color other than the whites and blacks.

She automatically searched for his fingers but couldn't get a good enough look.

Alex composed himself, swaying unsteadily on his feet. "My mistake. *Three* pumps."

The table burst into laughter. Nate looked set on violence.

"Are we OK to join you?" Charli asked, breezing past the moment and attempting to settle Nate down.

"Sure, if you can find a seat." Alex returned to his own seat and leaned in to whisper to Stacey. She giggled, then nibbled on Alex's earlobe.

Charli looked to Nate, expecting an eye roll or an acknowledgement of the discomfort of the situation. Instead, she found something on his face that looked almost like envy. When she scanned the rest of the table, the women were all staring up at Nate. Predatory, hungry looks covered each and every face.

Charli huffed and strode to a nearby table. "Mind if I take this?" she asked, lifting a spare chair without waiting for a response. She plonked down beside Alex, but away from Stacey, and nudged Nate to sit beside her.

"We need another," Nate muttered, tearing his eyes away from Alex.

Charli rolled her eyes. "Well, find one then, and sit down. Or, we can share. Whatever gets this dinner over with quicker."

Nate shambled off into the crowd. After a few moments he returned, barely able to squeeze his chair into the gap.

Charli picked up a menu. Pain lanced through her head, and she blinked with heavy lids. Although she had drunk a few small cups of water at the hotel, she was still dehydrated and malnourished. To top it all off, it looked like The Copper Bell had introduced a special menu for the weekend, removing all the delicious options she had seen the previous night.

If she could only order something that wasn't laced

with orange poison, maybe she could rebalance her mood and get into the spirit of the evening.

"There's nothing I want," Charli mumbled.

Nate exhaled loudly.

"Oh, I'm sorry, am I irritating you?"

Nate shook his head, his brow furrowed. "Not at all, *babe*. I'm having the best time with you moaning at every given opportunity."

Charli's eyes narrowed. "What did you just say?"

Nate's lips thinned. He cast his gaze on the menu then closed it shut. "I'm getting the pumpkin curry. What are you having?"

He made to stand and order, but Charli grabbed his sleeve and dragged him back down. "Don't bother. I know you'd rather be sitting here with your new fan club."

Before he could argue, Charli was snaking her way through the crowd. She waited her turn at the bar, swiping a layer of sweat from her forehead. She shrugged off her jacket, wondering how everyone else could be so comfortable wearing long sleeves. She couldn't spot a single person wearing a t-shirt or any kind of cami.

She looked for Donny. Unsurprisingly, she couldn't find him. Instead, a young woman with magazine-grade teeth and blonde, pixie cut hair balleted behind the counter, movements swift and rehearsed as she fetched drinks and flashed grins at the older men, all grinning stupidly as they waited patiently to pay. Charli eventually spied the waitress from the previous evening, speeding around the room with a tray laden with plates. Despite the bustle, she gave everyone a strained smile. Dark bags hung beneath her eyes.

"Help you, ma'am?"

Charli bristled. *Ma-am?*

Pixie Cut waited on Charli's order. Her smile was gone, a stern expression as Charli ordered Nate's curry, and a bowl of chips for herself. Her stomach rumbled again, and she wondered if she *should* consider broadening her horizons and eating something more substantial.

She imagined the orange pulp mashing between her teeth as a wave of nausea swept through her.

Pixie Cut gave Charli her change, then moved onto the next customer. The moment she turned from Charli, her smile returned.

What the hell? Charli thought. She looked down at herself, analyzing her appearance. *First the volunteer girls, and now you?*

She shook her head, attributing Pixie Cut's strange behavior to her own tiredness. Even so, she stiffened as she caught Nate beaming from ear to ear. He was already deep in conversation with a pretty girl, who flipped her side ponytail and played with her nose ring.

Charli closed her eyes, taking a long breath. She needed air.

Shouldering her way indelicately through the crowd, she found a side door leading to the restrooms. The moment the door closed behind her, the noise of the bar faded into the background. Charli followed the cramped and uneven corridor, past the bathrooms and toward a cool gust of air blowing in her direction. She found a fire door propped open with a bucket and mop. A security light above the door illuminated each streaking raindrop outside, making it appear as though a volley of needles was plummeting to the earth.

Checking over her shoulder to make sure she was alone, Charli plodded over and leaned against the doorframe. The air was cool and fresh. She closed her eyes and breathed.

Counted to ten. For a moment she allowed herself to believe she wasn't miles away from home.

That her phone wasn't broken and that her best friends were nearby.

That she'd found peace.

A peace immediately broken as a harsh voice snapped behind her. "What the hell're you doing?"

TEN

"Jesus!" Charli pressed a hand to her chest. "You scared the crap out of me."

"You've stolen my spot," the waitress replied softly, eyes narrowed to the sky as she exhaled a plume of cigarette smoke. "Crazy night, huh?"

Charli nodded. She held her breath, not wanting to inhale the acrid cloud. "Long day?"

"You could say that."

"I'm sorry, I never got to introduce myself yesterday. I'm Charli."

The waitress looked down at her feet, shoulders tense and drawn up to her neck. "It's not unusual. Most just call me sweetie or 'darling,' and I do the same. If I tried to remember the name of every patron who walks through our doors, I'd have no room left for my PINs."

Charli smiled weakly.

"Julie," the waitress said. "But don't go spreading that round. I don't want everyone knowing my business."

"Doesn't that come with the territory?" Charli asked. "Bar landlady and all that."

Julie narrowed her eyes, mirth pricking the corners of her lips. "I like you. I don't often have time for out-of-town-ers, but you... there's something... sort of... tolerable about you."

Charli snorted. "I wish the rest of the town felt the same. Can't help feeling like I've just picked up shit, climbed on stage, and clapped."

Julie almost choked as she inhaled her cigarette, her cough turning to laughter. "Don't take it personally, sweetie. People like them, they grow up together. We recognize our own. We know each other's kids and grandkids, daddies and mommies. Most folk in this place ain't stepped beyond our borders all their lives. I doubt any of them even know what a passport is. A holiday 'abroad' means skipping to the next county over, and even then, they'd hop back terrified that the city stink had sunk into their bones."

Charli shook her head. "It is different in the city; I can tell you that."

Julie drew the final drag of her cigarette. As she held the smoke in her mouth, she flicked the stub into the rain. After a long exhale, she studied Charli. "What's eating you?"

To her surprise, Charli's eyes blurred. She took a sharp inhale and looked at her feet. "I'm just a long way from home. That's all."

"And it's got nothing to do with that hunk of man you came in with?"

Charli met Julie's gaze. There was wisdom there that saw more than Charli was comfortable with.

"Husband?"

"Fiancé," Charli replied.

"Roaming eye syndrome?"

"Not before here. No. But now..." Her voice trailed off.

From somewhere inside the tavern there came a crash

of glass, followed by a loud cheer. Julie ran a hand through her flyaway hair. "That's my cue. Night like this and you'd hope you were fully staffed, but no... Hubby had to go and come down with the flu, eh?" She winked at Charli. "Come on. I'll get you a pie. On the house."

Charli offered a weak smile. "Oh, that's really sweet. Only..."

Julie cocked an eyebrow. "Right. The girl who hates pumpkin."

"That's me."

Julie laughed. The weight that was bearing down on temporarily lifted, and in that moment, the years fell away from her face. "Oh, you city folk. Normally, I'd call you guys freaks, but between you and me..." She leaned in conspiratorially, speaking in a hushed voice. "I hate pumpkin, too."

They laughed together, Charli for the first time feeling as though she'd found someone on her own wavelength.

"Come on, sweetie, let's get you back to the rabble."

"Sweetie?"

Julie winked. "Sorry. *Charli.*"

Charli smiled her first genuine smile since they'd arrived. "Would it be alright to have just another minute?" She nodded down the corridor. "Before I head back into the madness?"

"Whatever you need. Just no dine-and-dashing, please. We small time bars need every dime we can get our hands on." She smirked, then returned to the bar, the din rising at the open door before falling quiet once more.

Charli reached into the rain, water gathering in her cupped palm. The cool water was nice, and when she ran her hand across her face, she found herself slightly more refreshed. She took a long breath, then turned back toward the door, trepidation bubbling in her stomach as she wondered how Nate would be acting on her return. She already knew there wasn't a hope in hell of an early, intimate night together. Despite his promises.

She had only made it halfway to the door when she heard a clattering from upstairs. Beside her, a narrow staircase doubled back on itself, leading to what she assumed were the upstairs quarters.

Charli wasn't sure why she paused until she heard it.

Moans.

Not the good kind.

She froze, wondering if she should find Julie. Yet, even as she considered returning to the sweaty throng, her feet betrayed her, carrying her up the stairs.

The air was staler up here. Dust lined the lower edges of portraits hanging on the uneven walls. The doorways were short, as though designed more for large children than full grown adults. Charli followed the sounds, passing through another cramped corridor before finding a sight that defied logic and made her heart thump double time.

Scattered across the floor of a small storage room were dozens of pumpkins, some whole, some smashed and broken. In one corner, the pumpkins were piled into a large mound, reaching almost to the ceiling. Charli clapped a hand to her mouth, the fetid stink enough to cause her throat to constrict.

But that wasn't what dragged the gasp from the pit of Charli's stomach. No, that pleasure was courtesy of the two pale legs jutting from the largest heap of pumpkins—limp and unnervingly still. Atop the pile sat a single, grotesquely carved pumpkin, its jagged grin split too wide, eyes hollow and bottomless.

Slowly, impossibly, the pumpkin's head creaked around to face Charli and let out a low chuckle.

ELEVEN

Charli staggered back. One hand found the wall while the other stifled her scream. The pumpkin cocked its head to the side, that drunken, throaty chuckle coming from somewhere in the depths of its haunted grin.

No, not a chuckle.

A moan. Human-like. Muffled.

Charli's breath hitched. She peered closer, her eyes adjusting to the gloom. Through the small slashes in the pumpkin's flesh, she could see skin. Teeth. Stubble.

On the exposed forearm, a stained bandage.

Bile burned her throat. "Donny?"

Another groan.

Charli couldn't tell if the noise was one of recognition or of pain. She stepped closer, crouching until she was only inches away.

"Donny? Is that you?"

Dark, sunken eyes glared through the jagged slits of the pumpkin, empty yet seething with something not quite human. The crude carvings bled with stringy orange pulp.

The eyes beneath the mask fixed on Charli, then looked away as a more desperate noise escaped the cracked, peeling lips. Donny began shifting beneath the pile of fruit, struggling to stand up under the weight of it all.

"Hold still."

Charli knelt, placing her hands on either side of the pumpkin mask, expecting the hard shell to be cold. To her surprise, warmth and a faint thrumming pulsed through her fingertips, as though the orange skin had its own heartbeat. She strained against the weight, sweating as she attempted to lift the pumpkin off Donny's head.

With a grunt, she managed to raise the orange orb half an inch. A pause. A noise, slick and wet. Donny erupted into an unholy scream, the sound inhuman, a shriek that Charli never thought a man's throat could be capable of making. In the split second that the mask had lifted, veins writhed around the collar of the pumpkin, weaving through Donny's pale skin. Veins with a sickly green stain, almost like...

Roots. Vines.

Donny screamed again. Charli cried and pulled even harder, straining against a pumpkin that didn't want to release its host. A pumpkin that cracked at the sides and threatened to split, even amidst the soundtrack of the anguished Donny.

Charli let out an involuntary burp, a small hunk of bile making its way up her throat. She bit her tongue, eyes widening as things crawled out from beneath the pumpkin. Spaghetti-thin tendrils covered in tiny leaves, dripping blood.

Growing beneath his skin.

"What the—"

Thunderous footsteps. A shadow in the doorway.

"What the hell are you doing?"

Julie grabbed Charli's arm, stepping between her husband and the stranger who had wandered into their home. Her foot slid dangerously on a rotting pumpkin shell, threatening to spill her over. "Who said you could come up here?"

"It's... I just heard... Julie...? Are you *seeing*—"

"He's not well! Leave him alone."

"But..."

Spittle flew from Julie's mouth. Her eyes widened, wild and manic. "Get the hell out! Don't you dare come back!"

"Julie, I..."

"*Now!*" Julie pointed a finger, her face no longer the kind and caring mask of the woman she had spoken to downstairs. Charli tore away as fast as her feet could carry her, bumping down the stairs, taking them two at a time.

A wall of heady warmth coated Charli as she re-entered the bar. It was dizzying, a physical force. As she fumbled for the exit, unable to process faces or bodies, several heads turned in her direction. Nate broke conversation with one of the girls at the table as he spotted her. He rose from his seat, his face an expression of concern as he called Charli's name.

Charli ignored him, charging outside into the cool night air. Rain pelted her face, camouflaging her tears.

Before she could put distance between herself and the bar, a hand gripped around her wrist.

"Where are you going?" Nate asked, blinking in the rain.

Charli bit back a scream. "Let go, Nate. I don't want to be here."

"What the hell happened? I saw you go to the bathroom, and then—"

"This is fucking ridiculous. I'm done." Charli raised her

hands. "There's something fucked up going on here. You won't listen. Alex sure as hell won't. I'm done, OK? I'm fucking done."

"Charli..."

Nate's genuine empathy almost broke her. She loathed the way he looked at her, a slight tilt of the head, lips barely parted.

Charli wiped water from her eyes, hair sticking to her forehead. "Don't."

She took a long breath, attempting to steady herself, deliberately avoiding allowing her gaze to roam to the dark upstairs windows. Attempting to wipe the image of Donny buried under pumpkins and the sound of that horrific scream.

It couldn't have been real. That kind of thing didn't exist outside movie theaters and paperbacks.

But those vines...

Her head swam. Charli closed her eyes, trying to release the tension that knotted in her shoulders like sailor's rope.

"Charli?"

She sniffed, resigning herself with a self-deprecating chuckle. Knowing that, no matter what she said, no one would believe her. She didn't even believe herself. "You know what? It's me. It's all me. You're right. I'm tired. I'm hungry. It's been a long day. I just..." She blew a stream of air from her lips, avoiding Nate's searching eyes. "This is all my fault. I just need to be alone. It's just been problem after problem since I got here—the phone, the kids, Stacey, all this fucking pumpkin stuff... I just need a moment to lie down." She placed a hand on Nate's shoulder and attempted a comforting smile. "Alone. Seriously, you go back inside and keep Alex company. I'll see you back at the hotel. I'll... I don't know... I'll find some food or something on the way back."

"You can't go alone, babe. It's dark. You don't know this town..."

Charli snorted at the irony, and was almost convinced at Nate's sincerity, until his eyes flicked longingly back to the bar.

She placed a hand on his cheek. "I promise, I'll be OK. You've put up with me enough. Go have your fun. I'll see you back at the room."

Externally, she gave him a watery smile. Inside, her heart nearly broke. She didn't have the strength to tell him how she felt, or voice what she wanted to say.

She planted a quick kiss on his lips, nose wrinkling at the slight hint of pumpkin, and turned away before he could reply. Even as she walked on and distanced herself from Nate, from Stacey, from the bar and all its strange patrons, she wished he would follow. Wished he had the will to leave his new friends, to tap her on the shoulder, and tell her everything was going to be OK.

But when Charli rounded the corner, she became acutely aware that she was many miles from home, and the only person she could count on to survive this weekend was herself.

TWELVE

Charli walked under the glow of old streetlights, their frames black, crooked, and bent.

With the rain pelting down, she could barely see five feet ahead of her. The water soaked her clothes, her hair clung to her head, but she blinked the worst away. The only solace that Charli could take in being battered by the downpour was that it kept her awake. The stinging droplets drove her forward, one foot in front of the other, toward what she believed to be the direction of the hotel. Aching tiredness was a distant memory. She simply survived.

With each step, she shivered. The only semblance of warmth came from the anger that boiled in her stomach. At herself. At Nate, and definitely at Alex.

No.

She was overreacting.

Of course she was. Wasn't she? Phoneless. Friendless.

No.

Pumpkins. Thin green vines. That unearthly scream. Julie's fury.

No.

Something was changing.

Donny's not well.

Charli's exhausted mind conjured images of orange-stained fingers and leaves wet with blood. Pumpkin seeds masticated in hungry mouths. A loop of Stacey's laughter battered her skull as she passed rows of houses she didn't recognize, the cobblestones digging into her aching soles.

Donny's not well at all...

What was Julie hiding from her? What kind of bullshit was that? No one in their right mind would consider a treatment for sickness to be sticking their head in a jack-o'-lantern? What kind of cold or flu or virus would cause so much pain and resistance when removing a pumpkin from a man's head?

Charli sawed her nose with her sodden arm. As she passed more lightless houses she wondered if she was the only person out wandering the village at this time of night. Normally, she'd check her phone for the time, but...

Charli stamped her feet and screamed. Petulant, and exhausted. Her stomach roared back. Her hands clutching her pained, empty belly under folded arms. Her mouth salivated, and she thought of her bowl of chips growing cold on the bar table. Whether Stacey and her hilarious entourage had picked at them or if they were already too stuffed from their buffet of orange mush.

"This isn't what we promised, Nate," Charli whispered. "This isn't what we promised at all."

He'd never let her wander by herself before. It was one of the things Charli had always appreciated about him. No matter what they did, Nate was her protector. The chivalrous knight who doted on his future bride. For him to leave her alone in an unfamiliar village, walking home in the rain, no matter how much she had insisted...

And then there was Alex. Although Alex had always been more likely to get distracted and disappear as he lusted after women, he had never fallen that hard, that fast. Charli didn't like it. Not because he was her twin. No. She hated the effect Stacey was having on him. He was smitten, a love-drunk puppy that wouldn't stop following around a woman he'd barely known for a day.

Charli's toe caught on a break in the cobbles. She pinwheeled her arms, fighting to regain balance.

Fuck this.

She needed food. Needed shelter. Needed her room. Fast.

Her vision swam. She gulped down a mouthful of eager rain. Stared around.

"What fresh hell is this? Where am I?"

Standing in the middle of a crossroads, Charli realized with sudden clarity that she was completely lost.

Nothing looked familiar. The quaint, thatched houses had shifted to derelict shacks with tin roofs. The fetid tang of animal waste emanated from a nearby lean-to, and on the other side of the road was a large building that might once have been a warehouse, but now only had half a roof. Rust coated swathes of the corrugated iron walls, and ivy clung to its side, threatening to reclaim the manmade structure into the bowels of the earth.

"Dammit." Charli instinctively reached for her pocket. No phone. No surprise. A quick examination yielded no road signs, and as she looked back the way she thought she'd come, she didn't even recognize the street she'd supposedly just walked up.

"I'm going crazy. This place is making me crazy."

A shriek erupted from nearby. Charli flinched. It split the night, high-pitched and shrill, an animal's death wail, rising to the stars. Charli scanned for its source, adrenaline running a cold wash through her. She was almost certain it had come from inside the warehouse where a gentle glow of light limned the far edge of the building.

Charli took two steps back, heart hammering. *Don't do it. Remember the films. Don't be the first one to go. Don't be stupid. Don't you dare even think about it...*

Morbid curiosity pulled at Charli as she imagined the owner of that scream, scorned and pained, crying out for help. Would she really be the one to abandon them to such agony?

But, her exhausted mind reasoned, *what if it's Donny, or someone* like *Donny in there? What if they needed help?*

All the more reason to find out, surely? What if it was someone she had met earlier that day? What if it was Terrence or Abigail, or one of the bullish little shits who had whacked into her and broken her phone? Hadn't she been young once? Young and curious and stupid?

Stupid is the right word.

Charli clenched her jaw. Her nostrils flared. She took a step forward.

No.

Charli stopped herself, hands closing to fists at her side. It wasn't until she looked back the way she had come that her decision was confirmed for her.

She was no longer alone.

Standing there, blurry and half-masked at the farthest reaches of the rain, was...

CHAPTER
THIRTEEN

... J *ack.*

The name roared inside Charli's head, all Cheshire grin and eyes aflame.

She stopped breathing. She spun, splashing the pavement as instinct took over and she ran, arms pumping, putting as much distance between herself and the terrifying effigy as possible.

It can't be. No. I'm dreaming. I must be dreaming. Nothing I've seen tonight is real. How could any of this be real?

Yet the hammering in her chest and the burn searing through her thighs only confirmed it. Adrenaline tore through her veins, her mind splintering, spiraling. He was behind her, those flickering eyes sketched in the afterburns of her eyelids.

He was right there.

May still be right there.

Even now, skimming the side of the warehouse, she felt him closing in. Could hear his ragged breaths. Heavy footsteps beating the cobbles behind her. Deep, guttural laughter slithering through the dark, curling around her like smoke. With each blink she could see the light of Jack's blazing eyes, a jagged slash where his mouth had been.

Charli's breath came in ragged hitches. She wasn't sure how much more she could take. A door appeared in the rusted warehouse to her right. She fumbled with the rain-slicked handle, but didn't need to—luck was on her side. The door was already partly open.

With a quick nudge, she was inside.

A shove.

A click.

Safe. Perhaps.

Charli panted, back pressing against the closed door, ears cocked, muscles taught as she prepared to barricade against her assailant. Was he strong? Could a sack of straw overpower a human?

All these absurd questions spiraled through her mind as her chest rose and fell, water dripping to the stone floor from her sodden clothes. Outside, the rain pelted off the tin roof and metal walls, the hushed white noise magnified inside the seemingly empty room.

Charli counted each labored second until five minutes passed.

All was quiet.

No knock.

No attacker.

No monster.

No scarecrow.

Of course he won't knock. He doesn't exist. Sentient scarecrows aren't real, Charli. Come on, get a grip.

But, argued that tiny voice which grew ever louder, *if that's true, what was that thing I saw in the dark?*

She waited a few moments longer before summoning the courage to look. At first, by opening the door just a fraction. When there was no sign of the scarecrow—or anything else alive, for that matter—she drew the door wide open and stepped out.

Empty.

No sign he had ever been.

Ever was.

Ever could be.

Charli threaded fingers through her lank, matted hair. A flash of lightning lit up the sky. Charli darted back into the safety of the warehouse. She counted for the clap of thunder and flinched when it crashed, magnified as if the warehouse had harnessed the sound and doubled its volume.

"Well done, you fucking idiot. Miles from home, lost in a thunderstorm. Great work. This is how women end up as the subject of a documentary."

Another flash of lightning.

Charli closed the door behind her, sheltering herself from the storm. It was only then, as her breath caught back up with her, that she realized where she was.

"Oh, shit."

A dilapidated reception room. Darkness intermittently lit in camera flashes as the storm persevered, briefly illuminating a front desk, filing cabinets, and a threadbare sofa. Directly in front of her, the gaping maw of a corridor, with the remnants of an old door piled off to one side.

"Yep," she said. "This is the part of the movie where someone tears off my skin."

She made her way forward, slowly at first, her mind thinking of Scooby Doo and the gang avoiding booby traps in abandoned spaces. Always on the hunt for monsters.

Monsters.

Maybe it was a monster that caused that person to scream? Maybe it was...

Charli shook her head. She shivered, the chill making its way into her bones despite the welcome reprieve from the rain. She continued onward, finding a half-open door on the far wall.

And there it was. Again. A soft groan of discomfort.

Charli froze. Every cell in her body vibrated.

Once more. That sound. Filled with pain and relief.

Charli looked forlornly back the way she had come. Her stomach rumbled. She was weak. Malnourished. Exhausted. And now here she was, her stupid mind telling her to play Little Miss Rescue.

Well, it's either that or find a way to settle down with the roaches and mice on the sofa until the storm passes...

Charli stepped through the shadow filled doorway. She listened for the groan and was surprised to find that, despite the building missing half its roof, most of the external noise vanished when she took her first unsteady step into the dark.

She followed the corridor, arms outstretched, walking as a blind man would without his stick, making her way toward the source of the groaning, trying her best not to crash into any unseen items or obstacles.

She failed.

Charli's shin thumped into something hard and metal. She hissed, clapping a hand to her mouth, and paused.

Only that gentle groaning.

She tested the space with her toe and found the beginning of an ascending staircase. Moving painfully slow, Charli felt for the first stair, then the second. Soon, she settled into a rhythm.

Feel.

Step.

Brace against the wall.

Flinch.

Repeat.

As she worked her way to the higher level, the groaning stopped, and her skin crawled at the newfound silence.

Nate's not going to believe any of this, she thought, reaching the top of the staircase. *Not the storm, not Jack, not... whatever this circle of hell is...*

After a few moments and a few more stairs, she blinked. Soft light filtered its way through grimy skylights. Water dripped, invisible and constant. She stood on a metal balcony that opened to the large warehouse on her left, giving her a full view of the forgotten facility. Her shaking hands gripped the rusty safety rail as she looked down upon the skeletons of conveyor belts and defunct machinery, still and lost to time.

What was this place?

That question didn't matter. The thing that *did* matter was the movement. In the center of the spacious room, a bright spotlight formed a perfect circle around a large, wooden table. Three figures in dark brown robes drifted around the table, their movements slow and predatory, sharks scenting blood.

Beneath the cold, flickering lights, something writhed in visible discomfort against thick leather straps.

FOURTEEN

The grotesque figure lay pinned—a pale, naked woman marked by a web of dark, pulsing vines snaking across her limbs and chest. Where a head should have been, instead was a bright orange pumpkin, its carved grin stretched wide. Its eyes were dark.

On her wrist was a sparkling gold watch.

Shit.

The kids, that first night. The pain of concrete on her ass, the crack of her phone. The flustered mother running after them.

No.

Charli crouched low, terrified of drawing attention to herself. The woman groaned again, the sound muffled yet still somehow traveling through the abandoned space.

"Enough of your complaints," came a commanding, male voice beneath the hood of one of the robes. He was tall, at least a foot above the others, yet his frame was stick-thin, as though there was just no meat to his bones.

"You knew the risks, Sister. You knew the truth behind the legend... and yet you—no, your whole family—

succumbed to temptation. Still ate the poisoned seed. You only have yourself to blame."

"I still can't believe she did it." One of the figures lowered their hood, her back to Charli so that she couldn't make out the woman's face, only a set of broad shoulders. "I knew the children might complicate things, but she, I mean... Kate..."

"*Sister Parker*," corrected the first.

The woman reached a hand toward Kate, exposed and vulnerable, before the first cloaked figure slapped it away. "Do not tempt the seedlings, Sister Coxcombe."

The third of their company skirted the table until he stood on the other side, distanced from his two companions. To her horror, Charli noticed small fronds and vines emerging from the rim of Kate's pumpkin mask, following the man as flowers tracked the direction of the sun. He spoke next.

"I fear she is too far gone. We know not how she took the corrupted seeds, unless someone switched out her fake supply with their own, but..."

"Seeing it all up close," the broad woman continued, as though he had never spoken. "Seeing... This. I didn't realize... never imagined it would lead to..."

"This?" The third of their company shook his head, the paunch of his stomach fighting the stretch of his robes.

Charli's skin tightened. She *knew* those voices. Knew all of them. She just couldn't place them when her focus kept getting drawn back to Kate. A woman who, only the previous day, had been breathless but full of life, but whose skin was now so pale it was almost translucent, each vein a sickly shade of green.

What the hell have I stumbled into...?

The man with the paunch sighed, looking up at the

rafters. It was then that Charli saw him in perfect clarity—the thick beard, the rosy cheeks, the hint of a denim overall strap beneath the neck of his robe.

Farmer Stephen.

"How the hell does this even happen, Brother Ascott?" He said, his tone subdued, disappointed even. "How is it possible? This isn't what the Ring promised."

Kate muffled something incoherent beneath her pumpkin mask.

Brother Ascott brought his hood down. Charli slapped a hand over her mouth, biting her tongue, hard enough to draw blood.

That intense gaze, the wispy hair. Those gaunt cheeks, set on a face that, sharpened by the dim light, appeared almost as a skull floating in the dark.

The hotel clerk.

Only the day before, his voice had been strained, tired even. Now, it rang around the warehouse with crystal clarity, as if he drew on the strength of a thousand younger men.

"This is *precisely* what was promised. This is *exactly* what was described. We have fulfilled our roles perfectly. The activation agent is rife within the town, corruption is rampant, ready for His return. We, the meagre few, have avoided temptation. We, above all others, are not consumed by His forbidden fruit. If we do..." He motioned lazily to Kate's body. "This, will be our fate."

Charli gulped. What the hell were they talking about? An activation agent? Poisoned seeds? Forbidden fruit...

Her mind filled with images of white teeth relentlessly masticating pumpkin seeds. Orange-stained extremities and dilated pupils.

"Yes, yes," Brother Ascott confirmed. "There is magic in

the air. This is all precisely as Blue Ring's representative described. It was never our task to track our fellow brothers and sisters. No. Only to deal with the consequences, consequences such as these. Sister Parker has indeed fallen, but who are we to question His path? All is as it should be. We are, and will always be, blessed, so handsomely blessed, by His gifts."

"It *is* strangely... *beautiful*," the woman marveled, a strange twist in her tone as her gaze fixed on the dancing, reaching fronds. She slowly circled Kate's body, as if to test their skill. Dozens of tendrils writhing from the torn flesh at the base of Kate's skull, glistening with a slimy sheen, twisting unnaturally, splitting and curling in the air like twitching, severed nerves.

And then, in the harsh glow of the spotlight, Charli finally identified the broad-shouldered woman. The impish gleam in her eyes. The deep-set frown. The freckled cheeks.

Harley.

The vines stretched and flexed, reaching hungrily for Harley—quivering as if they could smell her, taste her. But the movement alone wasn't the thing that made Charli's stomach muscles tighten. It was the sound that accompanied their movement. A faint, wet squelch that filled the air with every twist and sway.

Eyes wide and fixed, Harley reached a single finger toward the tendrils.

Farmer Stephen tensed. The hotel clerk—*Brother Ascott*—remained stoically still.

Harley grinned drunkenly, mesmerized, the smile only slipping from her face when a single tendril snaked out from under the pumpkin, and latched itself around the tip of her finger. She yelped, recoiled, unable to detach the hungry tendril.

Kate groaned, the sound somewhere between pain and ecstasy as the remaining vines stretched their way toward their companion.

Harley flapped her hand left and right, up and down, fear coloring her cheeks as she looked to the others for help. "Don't just stand there, do something!"

One minute it seemed as though Brother Ascott would remain still as a statue, a morbid curiosity fixed in his gaze. The next his knife cut through the vine.

Kate shrieked, the sound piercing and shrill—or was it the vines screaming? Charli couldn't be certain.

The tendrils retreated, drawing back into the base of the swollen mask as a snail would retreat into its shell. Only a single vine remained, broken and weeping a sticky green residue, steadfastly glued to the end of Harley's finger. For a long moment, the vine continued to wriggle and move, until finally it sagged, and stilled.

"Thank you, Brother—"

Brother Ascott struck her with a backhand across the cheek. Her skin flushed red as a small, surprised gasp came from her lips. Her good hand moved instinctively to her face.

"I'm surrounded by idiots!" Brother Ascott swept in front of Harley, striking a terrifying figure in the harsh rays of the spotlight, the light accentuating every sharp corner and angle of his frame. "Are you unable to see the consequence of disobeying the Ring's instructions? Are you that eager to join the sacrificial fallen that you would willingly allow the vines to corrupt you? The representative was clear. We do not touch. We do not engage. We do not partake. We only distribute.

"The afflicted and those masked with the pumpkins will handle the rest. The seeds will lead them. They'll know what to do. Should you wish to join them, go ahead. Be my guest. Don't learn the lesson of Sister Parker and stumble around like a vacant fool until He claims you. That is your decision to make. I will not stop you or save you again."

An uncomfortable silence followed Brother Ascott's words, his gaze boring into Harley. Farmer Stephen looked between them, shuffling uncomfortably as Kate rolled her head back and forth on the table.

Brother Ascott's words were clipped and low. "We *must* obey instructions to the letter if we are to harness the power and release the idol. We are the blessed, and in the awakening of the power we shall receive our true bounty. Were these not the words that were delivered? While the town frolics and prays to false gods, losing themselves to the modern ways, we will continue the legacy of our ancestors and ensure conditions are met for His coming. His rising. His dominion." He closed his eyes, signing himself with the cross. "This time, Jack will not fail. And we shall be rewarded beyond our wildest imaginings. We are blessed."

"We are blessed," Farmer Stephen parroted.

"We are blessed," Harley muttered, casting a pitiful gaze to Kate. "But... we can't leave her like this, surely?"

A crash of thunder caused her to flinch. The others didn't seem to notice.

Brother Ascott held up his knife, examining the honed edge of the blade with something akin to lust in the hollows of his eyes. For a heart-wrenching second, Charli believed she was about to watch Brother Ascott plunge the blade deep into Harley's stomach and found herself breathing a sigh of relief when he tossed the knife onto the woman's chest.

"Do what you feel you must. I care not. For as long as we are all in the knowledge that the ritual begins tomorrow, the masked will lead the afflicted, and He will be free, this is all I need. Brother Harkham, are the preparations complete?"

"All is as needs to be."

"Sister Coxcombe, she is primed?"

Harley couldn't meet his eyes but gave a weak nod. Charli was alarmed to find herself feeling sorry for the brute who had contributed to the misery of her first twenty-four hours in Brackenholt. "She is primed and oblivious. Clean and untainted."

"Wonderful." With a flourish of his cloak, Brother Ascott stepped out of the spotlight and strode into darkness.

"Wait! What do we do with Sister Parker?" Stephen asked, calling to the shadows.

There was no reply. Soon, even Brother Ascott's footsteps faded into silence, leaving only the gentle hush of rain outside.

For a long moment, neither Stephen nor Harley spoke. They simply stared at the pale body strapped to the table, the vines having retreated in the wake of the knife attack.

"Do you think it's reversible?" Harley said.

Stephen's shoulders rose and dropped as he let out a loud sigh. "I don't know. She should have been more careful. She should have eaten the placebos." He drew out a clear bag of pumpkin seeds from his pocket.

"What if the children ate them instead? Maybe they're the ones who switched them?"

Stephen frowned. "Oh, God. The children..."

Kate grunted, trying to communicate something through the orange mask, her words lost to the fleshy strings inside the pumpkin.

Harley's gaze flickered to the knife. "We could try to cut it off? We could try to free her?"

Kate stiffened.

Stephen considered this, looking between the knife and the mask. "I don't know. I wouldn't pull it again. Those screams..."

"Cutting might be different. It might..." Harley chewed her lip. "It might be quicker, deactivate the..." She looked to Stephen to complete her sentence.

"I don't know what we call this. This isn't science. This isn't biology." He looked in the direction Brother Ascott had left, voice lowering, as if scared he may return. "This is... I don't know what we call this. All I know is that we've opened Pandora's box, and soon Jack will thank us." He nodded slowly, as if convincing himself of the truth of his words. "When he is released, our bounty will be given. We shall be blessed."

"We can't leave her like this."

"No..." Stephen threaded his fingers through his beard. "Jack will have enough tributes tomorrow without Kate, won't he? She was one of us. *Is* one of us. She deserves more, deserves better."

Harley nodded eagerly. Charli wondered what their connection was, how they were all linked. Harley had seemed so brutish, so emotionless during the daytime, what was this display of compassion she had for the poor mother of two?

Stephen cast one more look for the Brother Ascott. "Fine. But be quick."

They moved into position, Harley plucking the knife off Kate's chest. Stephen moved to the end of the table, hovering above her head.

Harley moved the knife closer to the pumpkin mask.

Even from that distance, Charli could see her hands shaking.

Kate was stone-still.

Harley let out a long breath, eyes darting constantly to the opening of the pumpkin where Kate's pale neck extruded. There was no sign of the vines, just a few, greasy stray hairs. She pressed the knife blade against the orange flesh, then sliced a long, shallow cut.

Kate exploded into shrieks, body thrashing against the leather bonds. Dark liquid oozed along the length of the incision as the tendrils returned, stretching several inches into the air before making their way toward Harley, unable to make it the full distance to her hands as they angrily examined the metal surface of the blade.

Charli clapped her hands to her cheeks, unable to look away.

"Hold her still!" Harley snapped as Kate twisted her head side to side. "I have to cut into the fruit."

Stephen grabbed either side of the pumpkin, the tendrils only millimeters from his fingers. He grimaced as Harley slashed a long line toward Kate's eye holes, moving with a frantic keenness to finish what she'd started.

A few more cuts and she peeled away a triangular segment of orange flesh, her mouth falling open as she tugged the piece free, revealing the mangled mess beneath.

Several layers of Kate's skin had sluiced off and attached itself to the pumpkin shell, leaving behind a rash of slimy, red skin. Twisted into the pulpy fibers of the segment, something long, green, and tangled hung suspended with a white orb clinging to its end.

Stephen gagged, hand moving to his mouth, choking back vomit.

Harley yelped, dropping the orange piece to the stone floor where it landed with a wet thwack. "Is that her... *eye*?"

Kate's eye lay still on the ground, several vines twisting around it like baby worms until they eventually fell still. The pupil looked outward, pointing directly up at Charli.

Charli shivered, lips moving as she mouthed silent, fearful prayers.

Kate stretched and contorted against the straps, the exposed part of her face ridged and messy, a wet papier-mâché project crafted from blood and vines. She groaned, cries growing weaker as her remaining eye looked imploringly between Stephen and Harley.

"What the fuck have we done?" Harley asked, wiping her stained fingers on her cloak to clear the corruption. "Stephen? What the hell have we done? They're... they're assimilating. The pumpkins... The masks... They're..." She looked at her hands, tears spilling down her cheeks. "What the *fuck* have we done!"

Harley turned and fled, her footsteps like drumbeats in the warehouse. Stephen stood above Kate, unable to move. Frozen in place, a haunted look on his face. His head shook slowly back and forth, gentle words on his lips as he babbled, "It's too late... It must be done... It's too late... It must be..."

Charli fought against her revulsion. There would be time for that later. She had to get out, leave, find safety. She needed clean air. This was all too much. She had only wanted to get through a quick, easy weekend getaway—a bit of alone time with her fiancé in a small, quaint town.

Now she was involved in... whatever the fuck this was.

Before she could move, a sharp *snap*.

Kate convulsed, joints creaking as her head twisted unnaturally to Stephen before revolving to face Charli as if she knew she was there, could see her in the shadows. Bile rose as Charli saw the detached eyeball join the intact one in an accusing stare. Charli had the impossible notion that it was still somehow a part of Kate, and that maybe she could still see her from the floor.

It was all too much.

Charli took several steps back, relief flooding her system when she could no longer see the horrifying diorama below. Her body shook violently as her mind raced to catch up.

Get out. Get out, now.

She was so close. She stepped back, but her heel bumped against a metal rod. The *clang* was akin to a gong, echoing and reverberating around the warehouse.

Charli's breath caught.

Stephen's voice, loud, angry.

"Hey! Who's there?"

FIFTEEN

Charli bolted for the stairs, feet clanging against the metal rungs.

Lightning tore across the sky, searing white into her vision, causing her to miss a step. Blind and reeling, she barely sucked in a breath before thunder crashed overhead—violent and merciless—shaking the very walls as she staggered down the first few stairs, catching herself on an unsteady rail made rough from corrosion and which grazed her bicep.

"Who's there?"

Charli's breath fled her lungs. She darted down the staircase, staggering and muffling cries of pain as the freshly scraped skin of her hands and arms burned with heat and roared in pain. Each step was like the thud of a war drum. Each stumble threatened to pitch her forward and tumble endlessly into the abyss.

Which way?

There.

No.

Maybe.

Another flash of lightning.

Stephen's urgent calls rang out from behind her. A door slammed. Pounding footsteps followed.

Run!

Charli was fast. But he was faster. She could hear him as she bounced off a wall, hidden in darkness.

What if Harley was still somewhere nearby?

What if Brother Ascott was waiting around the corner?

They'd surely catch her. Drag her back into the warehouse where they would strap her to a table until they decided what to do with her. Force feed her pumpkin seeds. Turn her into one of them.

Into Kate.

The masked.

From out of nowhere Charli stepped into something metallic and rigid, something filled with stagnant water. Her ankle twisted, the handle of a mop smacking against her chest as she crashed into the wall and slid haphazardly to the cold stone floor. She cursed, pushing herself to her feet as she shook the bucket free, not stopping to question what the cold slime was that now slicked her shoes and licked her ankles.

She swore again, limping now, until her hand found the doorframe to the reception. She fell through.

A crash, somewhere behind her in the dark. "Hey! Come back here!"

Charli hobbled across the room, almost catching her good foot on the leg of a chair. She shoved the door open, rushing back out into the storm.

She didn't hesitate. Didn't slow. Didn't stop.

A distant scream.

Kate.

Everywhere she looked, eyes littered the floor, her mind

casting images of a carpet of fleshy orange segments and detached ocular nerves. The ghost of the smell returned, invading her senses, taking over as she sprinted, adrenaline masking the pain that sliced through her ankle. It wasn't until the factory and the outhouses vanished into the curtain of the rainstorm that she allowed herself to stop.

Checked behind.

She was alone.

Charli bent over, resting her hands on her knees as she gasped for air, ankle hot and throbbing. Her clothes were soaked, frigid, cloying.

Then, despite herself, she laughed.

At first, it was just a disbelieving chuckle.

Then it grew into a breathy giggle.

Until, at last, it erupted—a raw, guttural roar, bursting from the depths of a broken spirit.

A roar that echoed around her as she stumbled off into the night.

SIXTEEN

Charli blinked. Her throat was hot and stale. Her body ached. When had she fallen asleep?

"Nate?"

Nate stood beside the bed, pulling up his jeans, busying himself in fastening his flies. He didn't even glance in her direction.

A crumpled blanket lay on the floor. Two misshapen pillows. Nate's bed for the night.

Charli's fingers gripped the covers of the bed. Her sore palms protested. "Nate?"

He grunted. "Thanks for leaving the door open."

Charli flinched. She sat up, back aching, foot throbbing, ankle radiating heat. She was fully dressed, her clothes wrinkled, the sheets clinging to her. She peeled away the cotton as she pawed her tired eyes, trying to piece together her thoughts.

"Nate, I..." She stopped, eyes glued to Nate's neck and collarbone as he adjusted his t-shirt. As a bright morning sun shone its rays through the glass, it highlighted the unmistakable stain of orange on his skin.

Nate didn't turn. Not once. He reached into his pocket, rustled a pack, and threw seeds into his mouth.

"You shouldn't eat those." Why was her voice so quiet and weak?

"You need to get dressed. We're late."

"For what?" Sleepiness shook off Charli in an instant, doused like a cold shower. "Where's Alex?"

It all came back to her, the night before. The bar. Donny. The argument. The warehouse. The hotel clerk—*Brother Ascott*—and his cronies. The creature on the table. She could have shrugged it all away, labeled it as some hallucinogenic dream, a product of her exhaustion, if it wasn't for the swelling of her ankle, the rough marks and stinging grazes on her hands and fingers. She had seen it all.

The tendrils.

The eye.

Kate.

After Charli had run back into the village, she had wandered for hours in the rain until she finally found the hotel. When she arrived at her room, Nate wasn't there. In one way, that was lucky, because Charli had their key. In another...

"Where were you last night?" Charli asked, hating how guilty she felt questioning him, as if *she* were the betrayer, and not the other way around.

Nate kept chewing and ignored Charli. "We need to leave. We're gonna be late."

Was his speech slurred?

Before Nate could reach the door, Charli stumbled out of bed and grabbed his wrist. He spun to face her, and in that moment she wished he hadn't. His eyes were dark, lightning streaks of red in what remained of his sclera. Bruised shadows hung beneath his eyes like wet garbage bags, and the tip of his nose and the lobes of his ears were stained in blotchy orange patches.

"*What,* is your problem this time?" Nate barked "Got something else you want to say that sucks the joy out of my life, out of this vacation?"

"It's not that, it's—"

"What the fuck did you expect from this weekend? Tanning on the beach? Charli, you said yes, didn't you? It wasn't just me and Alex. *You* agreed." He pointed to the door. "At least your brother knows how to have fun. We were out for hours last night, finally letting ourselves go. Enjoying meeting the locals. Enjoying *life*. Do you even remember what the fuck that feels like?"

Charli let his wrist drop and took a step back. Her bottom lip quivered.

Nate straightened, a look of disdain in his eyes Charli had never seen before. It was as though someone had peeled off his skin and stepped inside the flesh suit.

Charli took a shallow breath. "We need to leave this town. Please. Together."

"No! You go. Leave. At least Alex and I can have a little fun with you gone." He threw his hands in the air as he trod heavily to the door. "Fuck this."

Nate slammed the door shut. Through the thin walls she heard him knock on Alex's door. "Alex! It's time."

For the second time that trip, she didn't hear Alex's reply. Didn't hear his customary quip, jab, song, or dance. Didn't hear his door open or close. Only heard Nate's grunt of irritation before a single set of footsteps faded down the hall.

Charli ran her fingers through her hair, catching on knots. She stifled a sob as she looked around the room, as

R. P. HOWLEY & DANIEL WILLCOCKS

though there would be a handy local guide on how to deal with this clusterfuck of a situation.

How to deal with being stuck in a strange town. How to deal with being unable to get through to your fiancé, or your brother.

How to deal with knowing that your only safe route out of town was in your brother's Mazda.

A Mazda, Charli remembered with a sickening jolt of realization, that no one could drive without the keys that sat in her brother's pocket.

CHAPTER
SEVENTEEN

For the longest time, Charli sat on the bed, fists clenched in her lap, tears leaking down her cheeks, and thought of pumpkins.

The smell had returned. She found an orange stain lingering in Nate's blanket. It mocked her, kept a permanent fizz of bile at the back of her throat, ready to erupt like a volcano.

She had to get out of here.

But, how?

Cabs were too expensive, not that she'd even be able to call one. She didn't know the bus routes, or if Brackenholt even had any. If she could find a way to escape, could she really leave the men she loved behind?

When she finally found the strength to shower, Charli scrubbed until her body stung. She didn't look at her reflection through the mirror fog, choosing instead to turn her momentum to action.

There'll be time to read the story written in my new wrinkles later. In the grays this weekend has undoubtedly spawned in my hair like...

...tendrils.

Only once did she pause at her window, watching them from afar. The fields were crawling with volunteers, tiny from this distance, silhouettes of ants bustling about their duties for their queen.

Or their king.

As much as she tried to distract herself by scanning for Nate and Alex, her gaze kept drifting back to the scarecrow, proudly standing in the center of the field. A shepherd monitoring his flock.

She had to tell someone, had to find a way to draw people to this town. The police. The army. The government.

Anybody.

But... how?

She pulled on her jacket and left. When she noticed her brother's door standing slightly ajar, she paused.

Hadn't Nate knocked on that door?

Charli hadn't heard anyone leaving or entering.

"Alex?"

She knew straight away that he wasn't there, but it wasn't like her brother to not lock up after himself. He was freakily private, overprotective of his tech and valuables in a way Charli had never understood. He wouldn't have left them so exposed, ripe for the plucking by strangers.

"Alex?"

The smell was a physical thing. A warm blast to the face. Putrid, cloying. She blinked away hot tears. The breath she'd held whooshed out between her lips.

An unmade duvet was piled at the end of the bed. White cotton tinged with orange. Smears, staining the sheets. A gold earring glinted, resting in the center of the mattress. Packets and packets of empty seeds lay scattered around the room like fallen leaves.

"Calm down," Charli muttered. "It's not what you think..."

Her nose wrinkled at the faint whiff of a woman's perfume—a smell that was quickly swallowed by the overwhelming stench of midnight sweat and pumpkin.

"Jesus..." Charli muttered through her sleeve. "No..."

The final offense lay in the two handmade scarecrows strewn across the bedroom floor. Next to the effigy Alex had created when they arrived at the hotel lay a second, twisted into suggestive positions, as though they were both historical models left to depict last night's debauchery.

Charli sprinted back to her room, throat burning.

To the window.

Where were they?

There.

No.

She hadn't noticed it before. Her dogged fixation at finding Nate and Alex had blinded her to the others wandering around the field. The edges of her sanity frayed.

Dozens of figures with pumpkin heads, shambled around the field with slow, steady determination.

Brother Ascott's words echoed in her head, *"The afflicted and those masked with the pumpkins will handle the rest..."*

The masked...

My God. It's already begun.

EIGHTEEN

The lobby was silent. From where she stood, halfway down the stairs, she could see across the marbled tiles that led toward the exit. She strained her ears, determined to avoid Brother Ascott at all costs.

Each step was an effort. Every other step made her ankle complain.

As she neared the bottom of the stairs, the desk came into view. Aside from a ledger left open on the walnut surface, filled with vague scribbles across its pages, there was no sign of him.

Brother Ascott.

Charli almost made a run for it.

Almost.

Until she saw the telephone.

It was an old-fashioned thing. Black and suspended on a cradle above a series of twisting dials. It reminded her of something she'd seen in a black and white movie once. All she'd need to do is rotate the dial to the correct numbers, and she'd be in contact with someone who had zero connections to this pumpkin-infested town.

She thought of the only phone number she knew off by heart. Her mom's kind green eyes appeared for a moment before being quickly erased by the reality of her situation.

She waited another minute before stalking across the lobby. Even treading with caution, the marble beneath her feet seemed to be designed to magnify sound. She moved swiftly.

Reached the desk. Picked up the phone.

Her heart sank.

No dial tone. She tracked the black coils that should have trailed from the phone to a connection point somewhere in the walls and spotted the severed cable dangling just on the other side of the desk.

Had it always been cut? Or was this deliberate? Another injustice just for Charli?

She had no way of knowing. She only knew that she had taken her chance and now it was time to go.

Placing the phone back in its ornamental cradle, she half-jogged, half-limped across the hall, wanting to be anywhere else than here right now. The relief from throwing open the large wooden doors to the outside world was short-lived, as a croaking voice crooned after her, "See you at the celebration."

Charli turned over her shoulder to find Brother Ascott standing to attention behind the desk as if he'd always been there, a smug smirk sketched on his face. His gaze bore into Charli's, and for a moment they simply stared at each other, until Brother Ascott finally broke the lock with a dusty chuckle and began scribbling in the ledger.

Charli's heart hammered as she closed the door behind her.

She walked without thinking, one foot after the other, as gray clouds descended upon the sky and stole the sunlight. The alarm from seeing Brother Ascott had distracted her from her swollen ankle, but now it returned with a vengeance. She limped on every other step as her temperature flitted from hot to cold, failing to regulate as she faced her second full day in Brackenholt.

Has it really only been two days?

She remembered nothing of the buildings she passed or the roads she walked as she made a beeline for the farm. Had she been paying attention she would have noticed that every building lay empty, every set of curtains still drawn. The only relief she found was in the wafts of fresh, clean air, but as she approached Farmer Jack's barn and saw the masked and the afflicted set about her duties that relief soon sank.

There he was.

The scarecrow.

Jack.

He stood sentinel and unmoving in the center of the field, his head crooked as he considered his workers with soulless eyes.

"He's royally pissed off that you're late."

Farmer Stephen stood beside Charli at the mouth of the barn, so close she could feel the heat from his rotund frame. Now out of his dark robes, he struck a jolly figure, his rosy cheeks glowing as he surveyed the workers on the fields. He beamed down at her. "S'alright. Just throw on a pair of gloves and get stuck in when you're ready."

"I'm not staying," Charli replied curtly. She took a step back, keen to put distance between herself and the farmer. "I'm just... I'm looking for my fiancé."

Stephen's smile slipped for the flicker of a moment,

before returning with extra vigor. "Suit yourself. The positions are voluntary, we can't force you to harvest. I think you'll find the others pretty hard to convince away, though." He waved an arm, motioning Charli out into the fields.

It was a feeling she'd never forget, taking that first step outside of the barn. Framed by the open doorway, it was like a sketch from the pages of an artist turned mad. There was a static in the air, dozens upon dozens of workers fixated on their task, clipping pumpkins from the stalks and rolling them toward the crates. Had she not known what she now knew, she might have mistaken the carnivaled absurdity for small town fun, as she spied at least a third of the workers from the previous day now masked with pumpkins over their heads.

Each was roughly carved, the eyes angular, the mouths jagged and severe. Some eyes were wide, some were narrow slits. Some mouths were split upwards into devilish grins, others were downturned and sulking.

The remaining workers—*the afflicted*, Charli thought— tramped on, doggedly set to their tasks. Where yesterday there had been laughter and merriment, sweat and horseplay, today there was none of that. An eerie quiet carpeted the fields, only the occasional grunt or groan of effort could be heard as the masked watched the afflicted lifting pumpkins—which were impossibly larger than the day before— into the waiting crates.

Charli walked slowly into the loamy field, every nerve ending awake and responsive to the static. A stone's throw away, a young boy struggled to push his orange boulder, his face set with grim determination. A little further on was an elderly woman, her cheeks glowing with exertion, sweat clinging to her wrinkled forehead.

In the farthest reaches of the field, one of the masked stalked with long strides, inspecting the flock.

A hand clamped on Charli's shoulder.

She span, eyes wide.

"Cute, ain't it?" Farmer Stephen asked, cheery and without a hint of irony. "Did it themselves. Harvest moon tonight, so they wanted to get into the spirit of it. Festive bunch. Celebrating the legend of Jack."

Charli's lips thinned into a white line.

Farmer Stephen stood beside her, wrapping a heavy arm over her shoulder. "Honestly, you should relax a little. Get into the swing of it. Plant a seed of fun in your garden. Who knows? You may enjoy it."

Charli stepped away, peeling Stephen's arm from her shoulder as a waft of stale body odor came from his pits. "Don't fucking touch me again," she grumbled through gritted teeth, gleaning a small satisfaction when his practiced smile finally slipped.

She strode onward, driven more by her fear of Farmer Stephen than her concern of the afflicted and the masked. She scanned the area, desperately searching for Alex and Nate, until finally, after crossing one field and emerging into the next, she spotted a shirt and set of shoulders she'd recognize anywhere.

She couldn't see Alex or Stacey, but the other girls were not too far away as they slowly toiled at their task, Harley pausing and raising her head with curiosity.

Charli broke into a run. When she reached Nate, she grabbed his shoulder and twisted him to face her.

Charli gasped.

It was as if Nate's skin was glowing, the color of freshly applied fake tan. His facial muscles twitched, and as his head jerked toward her, clods of dirt and small bugs fell from his unkept hair.

"What?" he replied. Flat. Emotionless.

"What do you mean, what?" Charli hissed back, keeping her voice low. In her peripheries she kept tabs on the other workers, felt the heat of Harley's stare in front of her, Stephen's stare from a distance.

The others, those closest, worked on, unconcerned.

"Oh, Nate. We need to leave. Please. Where's Alex?"

"I told you to go." It was a simple statement, but it broke Charli's heart. Where was the joy at seeing his fiancé? Where was the affection? The care? The concern?

"I can't. Not without you. Not without Alex. Not without the car keys." She held his cheeks in her hands, looking imploringly into his eyes. "Please, babe. Something horrible is happening here. Tell me you're still in there. Tell me you can understand what I'm saying?"

Nate shrugged. Slowly. As though lifting his shoulders cost him more effort than he could admit.

Something thudded behind them. Charli turned to find an elderly man face down in the soft ground, deep tracks beside him from the enormous pumpkin that had come to a stop. His body convulsed. A few nearby volunteers moved toward him. For a brief second, Charli thought they'd help. But they simply stepped over his body and rolled the pumpkin, picking up from where he'd left off.

Without thinking, Charli ran over and knelt beside the man. She gently turned his head, the man's tongue lolling from the side of his mouth. She pressed an ear closer, finding his breath steady and rhythmic. Though he was clearly exhausted, she knew she didn't have the tools or the capacity to help him right now.

She looked around to see if there was anyone who could.

Her eyes locked with Harley.

Charli's lip curled.

Behind her, Nate let out a grunt, his face growing red from the effort of bending and trying to lift his pumpkin. His shoulders heaved with the exertion. Sweat stained his pits and the collar of his shirt.

"Jesus Christ," Charli muttered to herself before returning to her fiancé and standing in front of him. "No. I've fucking had enough of this." She pulled him upright, once more forcing his vacant eyes to look at her. His head wobbled on his neck, lips slightly parted in a gormless sigh.

"Nate, please, listen to me. We're getting out of here now. You. Me. Alex. We're going back to the car, and we're leaving. Now. OK?" She let out a pained sigh. "Do you know where he is?"

For a moment, Nate just wobbled.

"*Nate,* please. Tell me where he is."

Nate turned his head. Pointed.

Charli followed his stare across the field, past several afflicted, and past a handful of masked. It took her a moment to recognize the man's gait, the long, slow deliberate strides, and when she did, she felt the last of her hope abandon her body.

NINETEEN

"No..."

But she had no doubt it was him. The strides, the slope of his shoulders, the sneakers. The only part of Alex that didn't belong was the vibrant orange pumpkin that rested on his shoulders and masked his face.

"No... no... no..."

Charli broke away, staggering toward her brother. Across the uneven ground. Supported by numb legs. She fell into the side of the large crate as she passed, and still none of the workers seemed to notice her.

Pushing herself upright, Charli stumbled her way toward her brother, that "No..." leaking from her lips like rolling tides until she was there, beside him, and she grabbed him in white-knuckled hands, craning her neck to see inside the pulpy flesh of the mask for the human beneath.

"For the love of God, what did they do to you...?"

Alex twisted. Hard hands dug into Charli's clavicle. She ignored the pain.

"Can you hear me?" Charli's words were soft, unsteady. She hated the way her lip trembled. How tears stung her eyes.

Alex stared back at her in silence. The eyes within the eyes didn't blink. He took the slightest of steps toward Charli. She caught the soft jangle of something metal in his pocket.

Charli glanced down. Mud caked Alex's trousers. There were stains on the knees. When she looked back up, her fists clenched.

While the afflicted toiled away at their harvest, every one of the masked that were dotted around the fields now stared in their direction.

"Alex…" Charli managed, barely a whisper. "I'm leaving, and I need you to come with me and Nate. Please, if you're still in there, give me the keys and come with us where you'll be safe. We shouldn't be here."

A sharp, barking laugh rent the sky—*Ha!* Somewhere in the distant treetops, a flock of crows took wing.

Charli's neck twisted too far, too quickly, sending lightning up her neck, stretching the ligaments as she looked wildly around for the source.

There he was.

The scarecrow.

Inanimate. Lifeless.

But, watching.

Always watching.

Did he laugh? Was it really him?

Now, Alex was inches from her, head slightly cocked. A muttered *mmm-mmm* came from somewhere within the depths of the sticky flesh. His hands fiddled in his pocket, his forearms shaking as though fighting his own body.

Charli reached for the mask, wanting desperately to

release her brother from whatever unnatural spell had been placed upon him, but before her hands could reach his shoulders, Alex's hand whipped out and struck her.

Charli lurched back, dimly aware of the flash of silver slicing through the air before thudding onto the muddy ground. Heat blazed across her cheek, harsh, sudden. Her mouth fell open, unsure whether to laugh or cry.

Alex hit me.

Alex—the masked one that had been her twin—loomed over her, imposing. His chest rose and fell, as though he had just run a marathon. Closer, warmer, hot breath leaking from the jagged mouth hole.

"*Go.*"

The word was barely perceptible, but she heard it. An order. A direct instruction from what remained of her brother.

Charli became suddenly very aware of the other masked as they took slow strides toward Alex. She looked for Nate, but he had already forgotten her, his attention back on the pumpkin he rolled toward the crate.

"Alex..." One final effort. Charli wasn't even sure she made a sound before a masked in dirty blue overalls stepped closer.

He reached for her.

Charli jumped back, jaw clenching as her ankle twinged. She dipped, scooping up the keys that had flown from her brother's hands.

Charli ran.

Tears stung her eyes, blurred her vision as she navigated the uneven ground. Harley simply watched with a sad fascination as Charli tripped.

She pushed herself up. A haunting image filled her head of scarecrows chasing her from the fields. Of Jack springing to life, wearing her very own head as a mask. The ground sucked her shoes.

Another vision.

Green vines, reaching like fingers and hands, dragging her down.

Keep moving.

Get to safety.

Far from here.

Charli's did not slow. Not when she tore past Farmer Stephen who hadn't moved from where they both had stood. Not when she drew level with the barn. Not when she felt the firm reassurance of the sidewalk beneath her feet.

Through the village.

Toward the car.

Toward her only route out of her own personal hell.

It was only when the side cramp stabbed against her ribs that she slowed, huffing in oxygen, hands on knees.

She gasped, throat dry.

Turned.

There they all were. Rolling their harvest. Business as usual. Under his spell.

For a brief, exhaustion-fueled second, she considered going back. Trying once more to get through to Nate and Alex. Imagined herself grabbing them by the ear, or the eye hole, and pulling them along with her.

But those others, those *masked*. It was as though they were all working in unison. Somehow all connected. All of one system.

And in the beating heart of that system was a figure.

Inanimate.

Waiting.

Watching.

Jack.

She dug her hand in her pocket, fingers closing around the cool metal keys. She jangled them to reassure herself that she could finally leave.

It was what she'd wanted, ever since they'd arrived.

Ever since those kids had given her the first indication of how bad the weekend was going to be.

All she had to do was drive.

Just drive.

She would be safe.

Charli would be safe.

But what of the others?

Could she leave them? Abandon them. Resign herself to their fate.

"Fuck!"

Fingers still intertwined with the key ring, Charli walked. The streets were deserted, not a soul in sight. Why would they be? They were all down in the fields, preparing for the...

...celebration.

Brother Ascott's word came to her unbidden.

She paused, taking a second to rest her ankle, surprised to find as she looked up that the hotel was only a short distance away. She bit her lip, the small parking lot within sight. All she would have to do is climb inside the vehicle, turn the key, and she would be free...

Only a little further and the nightmare would be over.

Nate...

Charli ran her fingers through her hair, feeling the heat from her scraped palms. Her cheek throbbed. Her ankle whined.

Alex...

She couldn't leave them. Even if she got out, managed

R. P. HOWLEY & DANIEL WILLCOCKS

to find a phone and called the police, what were the odds they'd believe her?

Robes. Shadows.

Tendrils.

"This is all precisely as the Blue Ring's representative described."

"Shit."

How far did this conspiracy spread?

How long before Nate, too, became a masked? Just another senseless drone, tied and tortured under the gentle caress of Harley's blade?

No. She couldn't go. Not without them. Not without a fight.

Charli closed her eyes. Took a long, steadying breath. She wobbled, a little light-headed, but determined.

Afflicted.

Masked.

Pumpkins.

Jack.

"You've got this, Cee-Cee. It's time to show them how you bring the fucking rage."

Fists clenched; Charli stalked into the village. She knew she wasn't the only one in this backwater hell hole with a hatred for pumpkins.

She just had to find the other.

CHAPTER
TWENTY

The clouds unleashed a fresh torrent of rain, cloaking Charli from unseen prying eyes. Spurred on by rage and desperation, she made her way through the empty streets.

Hunting.

Searching.

Back to the bar. Empty.

Around a small, communal playground.

Empty.

Minutes turned into hours. The cobblestones pressed into her tired feet. With each passing second, Charli's determination wavered. Her search dragged on and on, yielding no signs of life. Anywhere.

Where was she?

"One more street. You've got this, Cee-Cee."

But once the labyrinthine streets and alleys started to blur into one and Charli lost any recollection of where she'd already searched, she'd all but given up.

Until she saw it.

The warehouse.

She shuddered.

How had she found her way back here again? To the edge of the forgotten world?

Houses with caved-in roofs decorated one side of the street, while an overgrown horse pen shared rotten, broken fencing with its neighbors. An industrial smell lingered on the brickwork, with smoke stains limning several buildings.

Blink.

In front of the warehouse. Unable to stop herself. What if Kate was still inside?

Blink.

Halfway down the corrugated wall. Sentient tendrils and screaming pumpkins. No... She couldn't possibly...

The door screeched on its hinges as she pulled it open. The familiar smell of rust and dust hit her, invisible fists tightening around her ribs.

So familiar, yet so different.

Her feet led the way, through the doorway, through the corridor, around the mop bucket and the congealing liquified remains. This time, however, she avoided the stairs and looked for a door into the central warehouse floor.

There. On her left.

She stepped into the center of the warehouse...

...empty.

Nothing remained.

No signs that strange cultists had ever occupied the space.

No clean trails of shuffling footsteps on the dusty floors.

No severed vines or tendrils.

Nothing.

Charli crumpled, knees kicking up dusty motes around her. Her hands found her hair, fingers threading through and pulling as she allowed herself one scream, one moment to let out the rage, the confusion, the anger, the pain, the torment, and everything she had bottled up over the last forty-eight hours. The warehouse cavern large enough to magnify and multiply her scream until the sound was primal. *Inhuman*.

She kept going, letting it all out, until her throat was hoarse. Until all that was left was a raspy breath. She stayed there, crouched on the grimy floor, breathing in the thick dust as gloomy shafts of light filtered down around her, the only rays holding her reality together.

They weren't there.

Had they ever been?

Had she imagined it all?

Was this some kind of hallucinogenic fever dream?

Would Nate wake her soon? A gentle nudge before pressing kisses against her neck?

She couldn't tell anymore. Wasn't sure she even cared.

Charli sat on her ass until it grew numb, her mind rocking with wave after wave of questions.

What was happening out on the fields right now?

How many more of them had become masked?

"Playing Jack."

How many more of them were falling under his spell?

Spell?

Charli let out a loud bark, the sound sharp and severe.

"Nope, nuh-uh. Not possible." Charli rubbed her eyes with the heels of her palms until they throbbed and she saw lights. "It's a scarecrow. Just a scarecrow. There is no spell. You're delusional. You need—"

A noise. *Click*. Stone against concrete.

Charli snapped her head up.

Realization.

This was her ending.

In the belly of a great manmade monster, the stomach walls stretched high up to the half-roof.

Charli wasn't alone.

Not anymore.

A shadow appeared near the door.

Charli stood, her legs struggling to support her.

"Whoever you are, just fuck off. I have a knife, and I swear to God I will fucking use it."

The car keys bit into the skin of Charli's trembling hand. The sharpest between her fingers. Ready to punch, spike, hurt.

A survival technique she had learned at school, oh-so long ago.

A groan.

No, a grunt?

In her mind's eye, Charli saw the body lurching toward her—a shadow tripping over its own legs. Naked. Alone. Scared. Confused. Yet it kept coming, drawn by her scream.

Charli's lip trembled. She tried to steel herself as the figure loomed closer, emerging from the warehouse's dark edges, until it stepped fully into view.

TWENTY-ONE

"Julie?"

But it wasn't. At least, not Julie as Charli knew her. The woman Charli knew may have been a little frazzled and overworked but still brightened up a room with her smile and mirth.

This Julie? This one was... ruined.

"Charli?" Julie staggered forward, torn clothes flapping. Charli ran to meet her, catching the woman in her arms as she collapsed. "Oh, honeybun, I hoped I'd find you."

In Charli's grip, Julie's body shook. Julie tried to stroke a mass of flyaway hairs behind her ears, but it was useless. Mascara streamed down both cheeks. A tangy smell pulsed off her clothes. Small chunks of pulp mingled with still-leaking cuts. And the bruises. Oh, the bruises.

Charli gagged. Forced it down. Gagged again. "Who did this to you?"

Julie lowered her head, her body juddering with sobs as the tears came. "I'll tell you everything I know. Please. Just take me somewhere safe."

Swearing under her breath, Charli looked around. There

had to be a better place for them than a dirty old floor in the middle of the warehouse. She knew from her own experience that anyone could be looking down and watching them from the shadows.

With some struggle, Charli helped Julie off the floor and carefully guided her to what might once have been an old staff room. Inside the gloomy space were a couple of plastic chairs that creaked a little when they sat down.

"Looks like my nephew's room," Julie said, a forced smile on her face. "Although this place is a little cleaner."

"Julie..." Charli didn't even have the energy to pretend to laugh. "Don't do that. Don't joke. Talk to me. What the hell happened?"

Julie dabbed at her eyes with a pull of her sleeve. "Right, I'm sorry sweetie." She took a long, shuddering breath. "It's the same every year... going back years. Morphing with every generation. A tale as old as time."

"I'm asking about the bruises. Not the—"

"They're not important. Just... you just gotta let me tell it all. Someone's gotta know the full truth."

Charli conceded, seeing how hard it was for Julie to tell her story. She bit her tongue and listened.

"Some call it Jack-o'-ween. Others call it Jack season. Others just decorate their house with his face or make little wheat braided versions of him for their home."

"The scarecrow?" Charli asked, despite herself, all the pieces of the puzzle flashing in her mind at once.

Julie nodded. "I know, honey. Probably sounds ridiculous to you city folk. Maybe even a little delusional. But it's a local delusion we all share. A belief—kind of like Santa Claus—that the kids love and the grown-ups revel in." She gave a lazy shrug, then winced. "Usually, it's fun. Each year the whole town goes to Jack's harvest, and when the moon is at its fullest, we celebrate. Oh, how we celebrate. Fireworks, bonfires, games, the whole caboodle. It's a staple of the Brackenholt calendar. One of the few times of the year the town comes together and pitches in. Kids run around with plastic pumpkins on their heads. They love it."

A memory of two children chased by their mother. "Playing Jack."

Julie nodded thoughtfully. "Aye. Playing Jack." Something dark flickered behind her eyes, an inner judgement she bit back. "I've gotta say, I haven't ever seen the appeal myself. Because the harvest often coincides with Halloween, a few of the more... immature townsfolk like to hollow the actual pumpkins. Wear them. Pretend that they're a real-life Jack. It's become an annual tradition for me and Donny. We play Jack bingo and see if we can guess who'll be first to don the masks."

The masked.

A haunting shriek.

Tendrils and blood.

Charli sat forward in her chair as something sharp poked her back. For a heart-wrenching moment she believed one of the masked to be behind her, until the ancient chair legs shifted, as though they might give at any moment, forcing Charli to brace herself. *Stay still. Let her talk.*

"But what exactly *is* he?"

"Who?"

Charli swallowed her retort. Breathed. "Jack."

Julie dabbed her nose with her sleeve, then attempted once more to organize the stray hairs. "He's a fucking scarecrow, honeybun. I'm not sure what more you want me to tell you. He's just a scarecrow."

"No." Charli knew Julie was holding something back. It

was as though she was trying to convince herself with her own words. "No. There's more. Please, be honest with me. My brother and fiancé are out there right now, rolling pumpkins, shepherding zombies like they're... high, or... tripping, or... I don't know. But something isn't right. They're not OK. And neither is Donny." She clasped Julie's hands in hers. "Is he?"

Julie's body answered without her words needing to. She sat back, body tightening as she shifted uncomfortably. Her lips thinned, eyes finding her lap.

"Julie..."

Julie took a long, steadying breath. "All I can tell you is what I've been told. What I've never believed. The reason for why this town even exists in a place that should have been impossible, but which continues to thrive." She rubbed her nose and brought her gaze to Charli's eyes. "The origin story of Jack, Brackenholt's savior..."

TWENTY-TWO

Centuries ago, long before the name Brackenholt had first been whispered, a single farmhouse, belonging to a farmer, his wife, and their dog, stood alone in the center of malnourished, barren farmland.

Day in, day out, the farmer sowed his seeds in the life-less fields. His back would ache, his clothes would ruin, and by the end of the week, he'd retire. No achievement, no food, with a constant ache in his gut at being so powerless to provide for his family.

Weeks passed. The farmer worked through the last of his store, sowing dreams that would never grow. Even when stubborn saplings did make it through the soil to peek at the sky, the local crows and ravens would swoop down and steal the sprouts. All the farmer's efforts undone.

Finally, the farmer's wife had had enough. She was starving, and the dog hadn't the strength to leave his bed. That final evening, with a skeletal finger, and sunken cheeks, she gave the farmer an ultimatum: find a way for his seeds to grow or live the rest of his life alone.

Spurred on—knowing his wife didn't make her promises lightly—the farmer left, desperate to tackle the impossible task. He roamed the hills, a ghost under an indifferent moon. He staggered across uneven soil until his knees were jelly and his feet were broken. When he finally collapsed to his knees, he clutched his hands together and prayed.

Prayed for an answer.

Prayed for salvation.

Prayed for a miracle.

Exhausted beyond even his longest days, he curled up in the mud and surrendered to tears.

When he awoke, it was to the call of crows. He blinked, unable to process the colorful blemish that rested beside him.

A pumpkin. Bright orange with a thick green vine knotting itself into the unfit soil, almost as large as his head.

Amazed and triumphant, the farmer stood. Tears flowed down his weathered cheeks as he spied dozens upon dozens more of them, none of them as ripe as the first, but all offering the promise of growth and sustenance.

The farmer laughed in delight.

Screamed his thanks to the sky.

Sank down and tore the closest pumpkin from the ground.

He ran excitedly back to the house. There, he and his wife celebrated with gluttony, eagerly scooping the flesh of the fruit until it was hollow—seeds and all. They devoured the fruit, juice and strings hanging from their lips. Even the dog ate its fill.

For the rest of the day, the farmer stood at the window, hands on hips watching his future grow.

Until he spotted a problem.

Up in the sky, a great mass of crows swirled, threatening to descend upon the farmer's bounty, oblivious and unconcerned with the lives they would destroy.

The smile slipped from the farmer's face as first one, then two, then dozens more of the winged beasts landed, twitching their heads and pecking at the defenseless fruit.

The farmer sprinted into the field, flapping his arms. But the crows paid no attention. They'd hop away, then return to their feast the moment his back was turned.

The farmer's hopes shrank. His nails dug into his palms. So close.

"Here!" the farmer's wife called from the door, holding up the creation she had manufactured from the hollow of the pumpkin's shell. A cruel grin carved into flesh, with eyes that spoke of warning. She handed it to the farmer who, in an effort to amuse his wife, placed it upon his head.

The crows took wing, fleeing to the sky in droves, terrified of this new aggressor. The farmer watched silently until they were distant specs on the horizon.

He removed the pumpkin mask and examined it, a smirk pulling at his lips. He placed the pumpkin in the field, staring up at the sky, and returned to his wife.

That night, they set to work on their creation. The farmer understood that he couldn't permanently fix himself to the fields, but with twine and timber, they birthed their first scarecrow, a mockery of man made from straw and pumpkin. With a satisfied grunt, he moved his creation to the center of the field and crowned the straw body with the orange head.

To his delight, the crows never returned.

And the miracles didn't stop there.

Under the shelter of their new guardian, the pumpkins grew and grew, multiplying into the neighboring fields with abandon. Without the farmer's interference, the soil transformed, and the area became the most fertile in all the land.

Soon, the farmer had more harvest than he knew what to do with. He reached out for aid, employing field hands, building extensions to his house, until a village grew, and their home gained national repute.

And even then, after centuries of change and development, growth and expansion, a thousand pumpkins have grown, eaten, and rotted, but only one thing has ever weathered the years and remained the same...

TWENTY-THREE

"Jack..." Charli breathed the words, enamored by Julie's tale. She could see it all. The farmer, the land, the crows, the dog, the scarecrow.

Julie nodded, her face somber. "Legends say it's always been the same scarecrow. The clothes, the straw, the head. Untouched, unchanged. The warnings, too."

"Warnings?"

"Aye, sweetie, warnings. They say, if the pumpkin's destroyed, replaced, or lost, the soil in all the fields will fail. Become barren. Our crops, and our future, will wither and die. Magic lies in that legend, Charli. Or, at least, it does, if you believe."

Charli thought for a moment. Did she believe in the myth? Would she allow herself to accept that the folklore to be true?

Yes. Yes, she would.

Wasn't that the point of fairy tales? The purpose of legends and myths? Sure, they were mostly fiction. Pure, impossibly imaginative fiction. But within each legend lay a kernel of truth.

No. A *seed* of truth.

"You must think we're crazy," Julie said, watching Charli intently.

Charli shook her head. "Not crazy, no. I mean, if you're crazy, I'm bat-shit insane."

Julie made to laugh, then stopped herself as pain flared across her bruised cheeks. A flush of embarrassment colored them further. She chewed her lip, hand gently rubbing her arm.

"Donny?" Charli said, finally closing in on the crux of her original question.

Julie's eyes shimmered with unshed tears.

"He's become one of them, hasn't he? One of the masked?" Charli pointed to her own cheek where a small welt could just be seen in the gloom. "Masked. Like Alex. He's one of them, too."

For a moment, a bubble of hesitation grew inside Julie. Grew and grew, until it popped.

Julie slumped with a resigned nod. "Aye, Masked, if you like. I thought it was all a game. That Donny was playing an extreme version of Jack. Maybe he'd lost another hand at the guy's poker night, and this was his dare. But the marks on his arm... the sleepwalking. I thought he had fallen to back to drink —seven years of sobriety down the drain. After you found him in the attic, I did everything I could to try and help him, but it was like the growth was part of him. I couldn't remove the mask. Couldn't separate them. Charli... the way he screamed, and the tendrils... it was like they were *tasting* the air."

Julie fell silent, silvery trails tracking down her cheeks. She shook her head and looked into Charli's eyes. "He's gone, sweetie. Donny's not in there anymore. He'd never hit me like that. Wouldn't leer at me like he didn't recognize me. He was babbling through the mask. I could only hear one word in his deranged whispers as he shoved me into the wall and ran."

Charli already knew the answer. But she needed to hear it said aloud. "What was it?"

Julie sighed. "Jack."

Charli's fingers unconsciously tugged at her hair, snapping the threads, snagging at knots. Relief in the pain. "Fuck!"

Julie flinched at the sharp sound as it bounced around the empty warehouse. What light there had been faded as small beats of rain tapped on the roof.

"How is this possible?"

"I don't know." Julie couldn't meet her gaze.

"Where's Donny now?"

"I don't know."

She placed a hand on Julie's knee. "Where. Is. He?"

"Where else is there for him to go?"

"The fields?"

Julie nodded.

"But... why?"

Julie's mouth opened. She hesitated, then closed it, looking down at her lip.

"What aren't you telling me?" Charli sat back, realization dawning on her. "This isn't the first time this has happened, is it? This has happened before. The celebration... Tonight's festival... It's where it's all going to happen."

Julie played with her thumbs.

Charli lost her patience. Fury, unbridled, surged through her.

Smack.

Her sore palms stung. Julie's eyes widened, then narrowed. Her hand found her cheek.

Charli's knuckles cracked. "It's not just Donny. You know that, right? It's Nate. It's Alex. I mean, it's the whole fucking town. Whatever you're hiding, tell me. All of it. Now."

Julie's voice was low, even. "Sweetie, if you do that again—"

"Don't give me that. You know something you're not telling me. I can see it—"

"I don't *know* anything!" Julie exploded, causing Charli to lurch back. Julie's eyes blazed. Spittle clung to her lips, and in that moment, Charli wondered if Jack had gotten to her, too. If Julie was turning right before her eyes.

But then she softened, as though fighting was futile, and all that was left was surrender. "Sweetie, listen to me now. That's all I *know*. Everything else is just hearsay and rumor." She met Charli's eyes, holding her gaze. "Some say this has happened before. A long time ago. Decades past. The last time the harvest moon met Hallows Eve. Under the same moon that the tale of Jack was born."

"What happened?"

Julie offered the ghost of a smile. "No one truly knows. One night, everyone was celebrating. The next... Well, the next, half the village had disappeared. Those who remained, well... let's just say they weren't never right enough to spin a tale again."

"Right," Charli said. "That's decided then."

Julie looked at Charli expectantly.

"Whatever it takes. However I free them. This pumpkin bullshit ends. Tonight."

CHAPTER
TWENTY-FOUR

J ulie led the way through Brackenholt.

The clouds were thick and the rain was relentless. A foul smell hovered in the air, one Charli instantly recognized. Thick, cloying, inescapable. She tried to swallow or cough—anything—but the feeling clung on. A constant reminder of what they had to face.

They arrived at a quaint cottage on the borders of town. Julie turned the key to her home, inviting Charli to follow. She traipsed through the dark rooms, barely registering the faded picture frames, the dying flowers, or the layer of dust which covered almost every surface.

They walked out through a Dutch back door into an overgrown, unloved garden. Thick, knee-high grass surrounded them, the low buzz of disturbed insects filling the air. Mosquitos, moths, and cockchafers, all busying themselves around Charli's head. She waved a hand at them, trying to focus on following, footstep for footstep, in Julie's wake as they closed in on a rotting shed.

Charli frowned as Julie plucked at a padlock, wondering how the house and garden had ended up in such a state.

She supposed working full-time in a bar was enough to demand their attention, but still...

The lock jangled lightly in Julie's trembling fingers. In Charli's opinion, there wasn't much point having it there at all. It could hardly be called 'secure.' The planks and holes surrounding the lock were so worn and warped that it wouldn't take much force for an intruder to break in if they really wanted to.

She let the woman work and craned her neck to the sky.

A swollen moon beamed back, an orange tinge around its circumference. Where had the day gone? How was it already dark? Charli tried to get a grip on her slippery reality. Failed. How long had she wandered for? How long had they been in the warehouse? What time was it right now?

All of these were questions without answer, and in a way, Charli supposed that it was best it was dark. At least in the darkness they had cover.

Creak.

"Finally."

Julie unclasped the padlock and let it fall into the mud. She stepped inside the shed and pulled a cord, a harsh shower of light dazzling their eyes as the naked bulb revealed a hazardous tangle of rakes, shovels, cables, rope, and a hidden kingdom of spiders.

She shouldered her way inside, stepping lithely into the sparse gaps until she grabbed what she was after. Charli left her to it. She'd already done enough. Too much.

"Ah," Julie's voice rang out. "Got it. Come here, will you?"

Charli did, inching forward, one foot outside, one in. "What's up?"

"Here."

In Julie's outstretched hand, a jerry can sloshed noisily.

Half-full. Julie twisted the cap, the stink of gasoline a sharp relief to the ever-pervasive scent of pumpkin in the air.

"Is there enough?" Charli's heart jackhammered at the mission they'd assigned themselves.

"I don't know. Here, hold this."

Charli grimaced as Julie, with perhaps more force than necessary, shoved the first can at her sternum. She grabbed another can, knocking it into a rake that fell and clattered against a series of plastic tubs filled with nails and screws.

Charli held the can steady beneath her chin allowing the fumes to dominate the scent of fruit. It made her eyes swim, but it was better than the alternative. In one corner of the shed, she spied the fetid remains of a pumpkin, crawling and shifting with insects.

Julie set the second can at Charli's feet, before plunging back into the mess.

"Damn, that might be all there is. It'll have to do. I'm pretty sure I've still got matches inside, though. Wait here."

Julie jostled out of the shed, leaving the door ajar. She traipsed across the garden before disappearing through the back door and into the house.

Not wanting to stay in the spider palace any longer than necessary, Charli grabbed a can in each hand and retreated. Grass whispered at her feet. Goosebumps prickled her skin as her eyes drifted up to the moon again. Even in that short time, the moon had somehow grown. The orange that had tinged its edges was spreading slowly, a reflection of all the afflicted and the masked Charli had seen that weekend.

Charli suddenly felt very alone under the moon's watchful eye. Somewhere in the distance, she thought she heard talking, heavy footsteps and childlike laughter.

Two children?

Playing Jack.

The ghost of pumpkin stink leaked into Charli's nostrils. She brought the jerry can close and inhaled deeply, glad of the relief, wary of the dizzying sensation that passed over her as the fumes fuzzed her brain.

If all went well tonight, Charli and Julie would save the town from this curse. If all didn't go well...

Charli closed her eyes, and all she could see was flames.

All she could hear was screams.

It couldn't end that way.

Wouldn't end that way.

Charli opened her eyes, a glint of rusted silver catching her eye from the tangle in the shed. She looked back to the silent house—no sign of Julie—then crossed quickly, reaching into the shed to retrieve the items from the wall. She placed them in her pockets, hiding them from view.

The back door closed.

Julie strode purposefully, breathless. "I couldn't find the matches. Best I've got is this." She held out a plastic lighter, translucent yellow. Barely a drop of liquid left inside. "It's not great, but it'll have to do." She demonstrated by thumbing the wheel, emitting a spark. A dozen attempts later, a weak light sputtered into existence, quickly extinguished by the wind. "It's Donny's. He reckons it's lucky. Won't throw it away. I keep telling him it's a piece of shit." She sniffed.

Charli chewed her lip, looking at the neighboring houses. "Won't the neighbors have anything better?"

Julie's eyes grew wide. "If you think I'm breaking into Lisa or Abbey's house, you're crazier than they are."

"It's not like they'll know."

Julie straightened, shoulders back, and took a long breath. "Sweetie, you're new to country life. We don't do that sort of thing here. Your neighbor's your neighbor. We look out for our own. Respect each other's things. What d'you think they'd say if they found out we'd broken in?"

"Gut instinct? 'Thanks for rescuing us from that strange pumpkin guy,'" Charli said with a petulant eye roll.

"Nuh-uh. I've gotta live with them. When this is all over, you get to drive back to your fancy metropolitan life. I'm stuck with the consequences. I won't allow it."

"And if I did it anyway?"

Julie's nostrils flared. "I'd like to see you try."

Charli contemplated testing Julie's resolve, but after seeing the determination sparking in her eyes, thought better of it. She barely knew the woman. Barely knew this town. All she knew was that she had to save Alex and Nate.

As Julie picked the padlock from the ground and locked the shed, Charli cast a sideways glance at her companion. A heavy feeling dropped in her stomach. A realization.

If it ever came down to a choice between saving her brother and fiancé or sacrificing them to save Julie and the village, she knew who she'd choose.

CHAPTER
TWENTY-FIVE

They marched side by side through the dark streets, Julie always one step ahead.

Charli kept an eye out for any landmarks or features that might have been familiar from her previous night. She saw nothing she recognized and wondered how big this small town must be, or if the town itself was a labyrinth trying to trap strangers in its midst.

The jerry cans sloshed in their grips. Each step amplified Charli's anxiety. Before long, the houses slipped away and the fields came into view in the distance.

Charli swore. Fires blazed across the acres. Long, dancing shadows stretched from the silhouettes in the distance. Bodies scurried back and forth, some still hard at work rolling their harvest, others gathering their winnings in unstable piles around the barn. The masked and the afflicted, serving their master, while two individuals in hoods strolled around and barked orders in preparation for the final celebration.

Charli pointed. "They're all there."

"Where else would they be?"

134

Charli bit back her retort. "This way, come on." She took the lead, her urgency increasing as she scanned for Alex and Nate.

The beaten dirt path led them both like a conveyor belt toward Farmer Jack's barn. As they approached, they stepped off the path, hidden in shadows, and crept toward the back of the building. Through small gaps in the barn's wood panels shone flickering light from a handful of oil drums, their flames meters clear of flammable material. Still, the proximity made Charli uneasy.

They skirted the building until they could safely see the fields but made certain to stay away from any light. To Charli's surprise, Julie leaned beside her, peering out toward the workers. "Where is he?"

Charli scoured the fields, her full attention divided between finding the grotesque scarecrow and identifying which of these shuffling zombies was her brother and her fiancé. It was hard to identify anyone thanks to the orange-tinted moonlight, and the fires scattered across the field which made the shadows lengthen and dance.

"I don't know," Charli said, gasping and ducking behind as a figure passed near them both and traipsed their way toward the open barn doors on the adjacent wall.

"Donny..." Julie muttered; eyes fixed on her husband.

And it was Donny. Or what was left of him, at least. The same worn jeans, the same tattered shirt, but now his sleeves hung in ragged shreds, exposing thin, sinewy vines coiled tight around his arms, burrowed deep into his flesh. Atop it all, his pumpkin mask, the one Charli had tried, and failed, to remove. His skin was stretched and splitting, raw and weeping. As he leaned forward, Charli's stomach roiled. A mass of green tendrils, gnarled and pulsating like exposed nerves, writhed up from beneath his collar, twisting together in a slick, tangled knot.

"Oh, my darlin'..." Julie pawed at her eyes.

"We've got to stay strong," Charli offered. "It's the best thing we can do, to help them, save them."

"But—"

"Julie, look at me."

She did.

Charli nodded. "Strong. Together. Yeah?"

A watery, tight-lipped smile. "Right."

Donny disappeared into the barn, for which Charli was secretly thankful. She didn't want to imagine Nate and Alex in a similar state.

They looked across the field. The distance seemed to stretch. Finally, amidst the shambling afflicted, she saw him. A lone shadow propped on his crucifix, idly watching the workers in their preparations. There was a strange, sickly, acid-green glow about the scarecrow that seemed to be growing as the orange of the harvest moon grew deeper.

"How do we get to him?" Julie asked, tracking Donny's movements as he emerged from the barn and wandered into the fields.

Charli's tongue worried her lip. She had had the same concerns, but knew they had two options.

The first was to set out into the fields and hope that nobody would stop them. Hope that Harley, Stephen, or Brother Ascott were so consumed with scanning their troops, they wouldn't notice the two women sprinting across the ground with their jerry cans.

But, they'd *know, wouldn't they?* She remembered the way the masked all turned on her as she had tried to get through to Alex. The way they all responded as if the masked were a single hive mind.

The second option... Well, that would require something that Charli didn't want to even think about, but which she knew she'd have to do. As far as she saw it, it was the only way.

"How're we doing this?" Julie asked, suddenly sounding younger than her years. "There are so many of them."

Charli stood straight as she reached down and tugged at the corner of her jacket. She tore off a long stretch of material, dipped it into the stinking liquid, then pocketed the sodden fabric.

"Leave the cans," Charli instructed. She took a step out into the open, sneaking quickly toward a large pile of pumpkins that were gathered along the nearby wall. At the bottom of the pile, a dozen or so pumpkins had been hollowed out, their flesh spilling from the hole as though the fruit itself had thrown up.

Charli grabbed one of the pumpkins. Without its innards, it was considerably lighter, though it still left her breathless as she placed one at Julie's feet.

"Yours."

Julie's eyes widened.

Charli peeked around the barn, waiting for another afflicted to disappear before emerging into the open and taking a second.

She ducked into the shadows, just as a bellowing voice called something indistinct. Farmer Stephen stepped out of the barn doors, his hood high about his face, but his stomach giving away his identity.

Julie was waiting for her, staring between the two pumpkins. "You're not thinking what I think you're thinking?"

Charli closed her eyes, swallowing back bile. "Have you got a better suggestion?"

"What if it turns us?"

Charli thought of all the signs she'd seen of people changing. Of orange fingers and orange noses. Dark vines and irremovable pumpkin masks. She thought back to the warehouse, to the robed freaks' conversation and their talk of poisoned seeds.

"It's not the pumpkins," Charli replied. "It's the seeds. It's the produce. You said it yourself. You hate pumpkins. I hate pumpkins. We haven't eaten what the rest of them have. These are just... masks. Protection."

Julie wasn't convinced. "What if you're wrong?"

"Then we take them off. At the first sign of something freaky, we take them off. OK?"

Julie swallowed. "You first."

Charli raised hers in shaking arms. She stared for a moment into the opening, at the stringy flesh and slimy sides. The smell struck her with ferocity, and for a moment she doubted that she could do it, that the pumpkin would only end up acting as a receptacle for her vomit.

"For Donny," Julie stated. "For Alex and Nate."

Charli took a deep breath, then placed on her mask. It was cold and gooey. Strings of innards clung to her skin, their juice dampening her hair. She convulsed, trying to bring a hand to her mouth but accidentally hitting pumpkin shell.

She opened her eyes and only found orange darkness. "There's no holes. There are no holes to breathe! I can't..."

Rough hands grabbed her head. Spun the pumpkin around. The strings and juices slimed across her face until two crude eye holes and a wide mouth appeared before her. Her senses were overwhelmed, eyes wide as Julie's face appeared inside her own pumpkin mask.

"It's OK, sweetie," Julie soothed, placing her hands on

Charli's shoulders. "That's better, ain't it? There. Don't think about it. Let's do this. Let's go, before it's too late."

"Right," Charli managed between sharp breaths, trying her best not to take in the smell and taste if she could help it. "OK. We've got this."

She faced the fields. After a quick inspection to ensure that Farmer Stephen had moved on, they took their first steps into the open. "Even strides, Julie. Don't make eye contact if you can help it."

Julie didn't reply, but Charli felt her close behind. A few short seconds later, they were in the field, away from the bright lights of the open barn doors and lit from above by the moon's ochre glow.

The ground shifted treacherously beneath Charli's feet, each step sinking into the soft, tilled earth. She hardly dared breathe as villagers drifted past, hollow-eyed and slack-jawed; their movements mechanical, methodical. Dark shadows clung beneath their eyes, and strings of drool glistened on a few chins as they mindlessly rolled bloated pumpkins toward the looming barn.

No one looked toward them.

No one paid attention.

Charli's concerns shifted from the masked to the hooded three. With her limited vision, she couldn't gain a full view of the surrounding fields, and she hoped that if Julie saw any of them she might get a tap on the shoulder or some advanced warning. Whatever the consequence, it was Jack that they gunned for.

"Shit!" Charli's ankle gave, finding a small divot in the mud. Her already sore joint twisted sharply, lurching her forward. Julie's arms caught her just in time. A hiss escaped her lips and she breathed in a dangling string of pumpkin flesh. She coughed, doing her best to hold it all in, but failing.

"We're so close, Charli. Just a little further."

But Charli didn't move.

Not just because of the pain and the boil of bile in her throat, but because someone was staring at her, only a few meters away.

Nate.

Charli stared into the lifeless eyes of her fiancé. He swayed as he stood, eyes unregistering beneath the guise of his newly bequeathed pumpkin mask. Her heart stopped as he looked in her direction, his trousers caked in mud, his shirt ruined.

Go to him. Save him, Charli. He needs you.

"Oh, my God... Nate... No... Not you, too..."

"Listen," Julie urged, hands pressing into Charli's back as an eerie quiet fell around them. "We have to destroy Jack to save him."

Charli swallowed.

Blinked.

Nodded.

The first step was the hardest, pulling herself away from Nate, wondering if it was already too late. The second was the most painful, her ankle feeling as though the bones were made of sponge.

They were so close.

The scarecrow was only a short distance from them, bone idle and waiting, that ghastly green aura rolling off his shape like smoke.

The silence deepened.

The masked were the first to turn.

The afflicted followed shortly after, dozens upon dozens of heads turning in unison to face the intruders.

Charli made a break for it, adrenaline cloaking the pain in her ankle. Julie followed.

Arms pumping, Charli sped toward Jack, closing the last of the distance. She ripped the mask off her head, leaving it to roll in the soil, all pretense abandoned.

Her only chance.

Destroy the head.

The only way.

Destroy the head, and the rest would fall. Whatever cosmic curse had gripped the town would break, and future generations would be safe.

The masked and the afflicted shambled closer, closer, always closer.

Among the front lines, Nate, grunting and pointing, his carved grin wide and triumphant.

Charli reached Jack, pulling to an abrupt halt in front of the scarecrow. Her neck complained as she stared up, up, up into his demonic face. Dark, lifeless eyeholes. An empty grin, barren and gaping. For the faintest of moments, Charli was aware how absurd all of this seemed.

Until the green glow brightened, flaring like an eager fire.

Charli drew the fuel-soaked rag from inside her jacket. She thrust the cloth into the cavern of Jack's leering mouth.

Was that... laughter?

"Here!"

Julie thrust the lighter into Charli's hand. She thumbed the wheel, the metal spinning, flint sparking.

Julie muttered mumbled prayers.

Flick, click.

Flick, click.

No flame.

Charli screamed. "Please, please, please, please... Please you *son of a bitch*!"

Something crackled in the clouds, a rogue flash of lightning.

No thunder.

Julie whimpered.

Silence fell.

Charli kept trying, blistering her thumb, shaving off skin until—

"A-ha!"

A flame, weak and meager. Charli made to ignite the damp rag, when a gust of wind blew sharply across them, extinguishing the flame.

A split second's pause.

Light flooded her face as flames erupted from Jack's hollow eyes, the unnatural embers racing to eat up the cloth as a haunting laugh sprang from the gaping maw, drawing in the rag like a serpent's flicking tongue.

Something sharp and heavy struck Charli from behind.

And all she knew was darkness.

TWENTY-SIX

Charli tried to open her eyes, but her lashes wouldn't let her. Blistering pain pulsed through her skull.

She tried again. Something sticky, blurred her vision. Her nostrils flared. The earthy smell of hay mixed with the musty scent of old wood, and that ever-pervasive stench of pumpkin created a heady concoction that made her heart pound.

She tried to move.

Couldn't.

Where am I?

She attempted to blink. Once. Twice. The sticky substance split.

Dark crimson.

Blood.

Where am I?

Her breaths came shallow, rapid, as light danced in her eyes. She forced herself to calm. Deep breath in, deep breath out.

Something irritated her gums. She turned her head sideways, spitting out hay. Every inch of her body ached. With each dizzied movement something coarse and unyielding scratched her skin.

Shit.

It all came back to her with a sudden spike of adrenaline. She strained against the bindings holding her in place, thick rope that bound tightly around her chest, wrists, ankles, burning with the friction of movement.

Neck straining, she managed to look around. She was on a raised bed of hay, but something sharp pressed into the length of her spine, along her outstretched arms, and her numb legs.

No, no, no, no...

Realization dawned as she focused on the shape of her trapped limbs. Arms out to each side, legs together, ankle bones pressing painfully against each other. A makeshift crucifix. Bound in place like the Holy Christ.

But her flock wasn't human.

Not really.

They surrounded her, terrifying and warped, stoic and soundless in the half-shadows cast by the few small candles smoldering dangerously close to her pyre of hay.

"No..." Charli croaked. "Please. Let me go."

No one moved. A carnival of twisted mannequins or dolls in a possessed child's ritual. Staring, unblinking.

Masked stared at her with dark eyes, no signs of the used-to-be humans beneath. The smell overpowered her. Her back arched as she belched, thick bile dribbling down the side of her mouth, slopping onto the hay.

Why was no one moving?

Their bodies were packed tight, shoulder to shoulder, an immovable force. Overhead, legs dangled from the ancient beams of the barn's roof as more of them stared down. Were it not for the bright orange moonlight that shone through the gaps in the barn's roof, and the surrounding candles, Charli might have missed them.

One of them shifted, a gentle rain of dust and splinters showering down as a shadow appeared before Charli. At her feet stood a robed figure, tall and thin. Charli didn't need Brother Ascott to remove his hood to recognize his skeletal features, the hollows of his eyes and the dip of his cheeks.

"What the fuck are you doing, you sick bastard?" Charli managed, the fire of her spirit lighting as panic set in. "This is your fault. All of this. I saw you, you... *psychopath*. What did you give them?" She was practically screaming now. "What the fuck have you done!"

Her fury surged as he smiled. Clasping his hands in front of him, he walked slowly around Charli until he was standing beside her chest, looking down into her eyes. Charli thrashed, grunting and moaning as she fought to free herself from her bonds, but only managing to make her skin red.

Brother Ascott leaned close, only a whisper away. "You'd do well to lay still and obey, little girl. All will be over soon. He promises it to you."

"Who?" Charli asked. She already knew, but even in her final moments, she refused to acknowledge it. Standing on the precipice between reality and impossibility, she refused to take the final step. Wouldn't allow herself to voluntarily plunge into the madness, the chaos.

Brother Ascott smiled again, a toothy, gummy smile, filled with the promise of enlightenment and suffering. Didn't respond.

It didn't matter.

He didn't have to.

Because He'd already arrived.

TWENTY-SEVEN

His laughter was the shrill cackle of a broken lawn mower. His voice was jovial, loud, obnoxious, a caricature of an animated children's character.

"Oh, how *wonderful*!" Jack sang, reminding Charli of a clown, standing before a crowd of children at a party, telling them to pay attention, to quiet down. "Oh, how *blessed*!"

His followers shifted, making way for the impossible figure emerging through the main barn doors. The temperature dropped. Charli's breath misted before her eyes. Hay, leaves, and detritus tumbled across the floor as a harvest-laced breeze filled the room.

He stalked toward her, head bobbing absurdly from left to right, as if the man-made straw neck wasn't built to support its weight. Long, dangling arms, thick in some places, thin in others, swung beside the misshapen body. He stepped into the center of the crowd.

One of the masked reached for Jack with unsteady arms.

He slapped it away like a cow's tail to the fly.

"I cannot *tell* you how wonderful it is to be free. All those years, years and years and *years*, strung up and waiting on that horrid cross. It's enough to give you backache," he stretched back to an inhuman angle, grinning at Charli. "Wouldn't you agree?"

Charli's lip quivered; words scurrying up her throat, but not as fast as the creature that dashed in the blink of an eye.

One minute he was before her, then he was gone in a puff of acrid green smoke. A moment later, he reappeared behind a thick structural beam, his thin fingers gripping the wood as he peered toward her. The crowd moved back, melting into the background, giving Jack center stage.

Charli blinked. Green smoke. Gone again.

In front of her.

Charli couldn't breathe—didn't want to inhale his fumes. Time stretched, impossibly slow. Charli whimpered. Jack stared. His arms quivered, and from deep within one crudely stitched pocket something fidgeted, a long vine briefly licking the air before disappearing.

He giggled, a broken, corrupted sound. "You have no idea how good it feels to be free, my dear. How good it feels to *streeeetch*."

Here, Jack tested his arms, flexing once again as he twisted his head in a full rotation, much to the drunken delight of the onlookers. Several villagers chuckled softly. A few maskless drooled as their mouths broke into clumsy smiles. Charli looked to Nate, finding him staring vacantly, not an ounce of recognition on his face.

Nearby, Brother Ascott stood with a rictus grin, eyes wide in wonder.

Is this real? How is any of this real?

Another low whimper tore its way from Charli's throat, and Jack's glowing, fiery eyes fixed on her.

Another bob, a gentle wobble.

Jack collapsed.

Picked himself up.

A deer learning to walk.

"*Oops!* Clumsy me. It's a strange phenomenon, you must agree," Jack said, "But one I've looked forward to savoring for longer than you care to imagine. The rare, undulating power of the harvest and the hallows—delicious. Can you taste it?" His head tilted, and his eyes pulsed. "Tastes like... promise. Retribution, even.

"I have waited. I have watched. I have fertilized this ground, and I alone kept the vermin at bay. This is my time. Not yours, not theirs... mine."

With a cackle, he bent and jumped, twisting and writhing through the air. He landed astride Charli with a solid thump, slammed his arms down on either side of her head, blazing eyes inches before hers until all she could see was fire. All she could smell was his fruit.

"You are the strongest, my dear. The strongest among them. The only one truly unaffected by the seeds I sowed." He cocked his head, eyes blazing with curiosity. "But you see, my dearest, even those who claimed to be loyal could not resist."

His gaze flickered to the corner of the barn, and to Charli's horror, in the darkest shadows, she could make out a pale, naked body. Slumped. Covered in vines. A golden watch on a limp wrist. A pumpkin where a head should have been, rotten and collapsing.

"Yes, yes," Jack continued. "They said a clean one wouldn't come, but you resisted, didn't you? Of all the people that could have been chosen as proxy, it's you..." He barked a laugh that stung Charli's ears, eyes blazing, before suddenly it died, and he drew closer, pumpkin shell touching nose. "Still, it's curious... One so young as you. One so... *determined*. But fresh and ready, yes... and just the right size, too."

Charli swallowed thickly, unable to blink, unwilling to look away. "What do you want from me?"

Jack grinned, the crude carvings of his mouth stretching so wide that Charli wondered if his jaw would hinge off. "Why, I need someone to take my place, of course."

"For centuries I stood sentinel," Jack announced, sitting upright and addressing his congregation. "Countless efforts, countless plans. To free myself, to roam the world unrooted. All of them thwarted. Every time. Decades between and always lying in wait. But not this time. No... Thanks to my friends I have this chance. Thanks to you... I have... the greatest possibility of freedom." He returned to her, crouching low. Something shifted in the strands between the straw, and Charli was certain she saw a long pink tail disappear inside. "Can you imagine what it's like, standing there day after day? Bracing against the wind, the rain, the snow. Melting in the summer sun." He snorted. "Well, you'll know soon enough, my dear. It's hardly a picnic."

Charli whimpered. Beside her, unnoticed, something shifted.

"But... I saw you. You moved. There and then gone. Back again."

"Oh, I had my accomplices, sweetness. I had my stooges."

Charli looked past Jack to the triumphant Brother Ascott. Her fists clenched. At Brother Ascott's side, the others, hooded and cloaked. Silent. Waiting.

"As the harvest moon approaches, I learn to speak again. As the harvest moon zeniths, I learn to move again. Without my accomplices we couldn't have conspired. Couldn't have pulled this together. Couldn't have placed you in the heart of our desires." He paused, touching a bracken finger to his lips, avoiding the flame. "Well, it was either you or her, and I think you stood the much better chance of acting as conduit."

Julie stepped forward as if summoned by an indirect order. Her leg dragged, her eyes were vacant. Her mouth hung open with a long string of drool falling to the neck of her torn shirt.

"Julie..." Charli managed.

"You've heard those twisted tales, haven't you?" Jack pressed on, undeterred. "Those hateful yarns, wending and winding their way through time. Fairy tales. Myths. Legends. *PAH!* Cancerous ideals. Filled with unfounded hope. That's why you tried to burn me, wasn't it? *PAH-PAH!* A futile gesture. That's not where the magic lies, you know. The magic lies deep within here." Jack tapped the side of his head, leaning back enough to allow Charli a moment to breathe. "And now, here we are, and the moon is high and the harvest is nearly complete."

It happened without warning. Jack let out a shotgun *PAH!*

His lips parted and spewed forth a viscous, pulpy substance.

Jack's bile shot forth in a torrent, covering Charli's face, clogging her nostrils, cutting off her airways. It flowed over her like an undercurrent, pulling and tossing as she thrashed her head side to side to escape the worst of the mixture.

And in the darkness of her eyelids, Charli retreated to her childhood.

Bowls and bowls of pulp, dozens of empty pumpkins. Seeds.

Her mother, ladle in hand, sweating and singing to herself, busying herself with preparing the festivities for the local youth center.

Carving, so much carving. Cooking. Pies and sweet treats. Demanding Charli taste and taste until she felt sick. Taste and taste until Charli was full.

Nights spent scrubbing the sticky residue from juvenile palms. Nights spent retching and releasing it all back into the stale water in the bowl. Her mother's anger. The welts from wooden spoons struck against the back of legs.

Another spoonful, forcing it down. Punishment. Retribution. Stomach churning, swallowing bile. Her mother's smile.

Alex staring at her with concern from the doorway, too young for his voice to be heard as sweat pooled in Charli's armpits and she fought back tears.

PAH!

Charli fought for breath, spitting and spluttering beneath Jack's wet belches.

And then, when it seemed like Charli could take no more, it stopped.

"Look at me, sweetness, look at me!"

Charli spat, chest heaving. As much as she tried to avoid it, globs of pumpkin stuck to her lips. It was in her nose, slimed her eyes. Charli shook her head, blinking away the stinging substance until she could just about see.

Jack bellowed his laughter, springing into the air as he launched off Charli in a single bound. He turned to his flock. "Ladies. Gentlemen." He doffed his head toward Kate's corpse in the corner. "The deceased... it is *time!*"

He clapped his mockery of hands and motioned for the devoted to step forward. The cloaked ones moved silently, grabbing the crucifix in steady hands.

Only a short distance away, Nate watched, unblinking.

"Nate! Nate, please! Help me. If you're in there. If there's *any* part of you still—" She coughed, choking on a seed which she managed to spit across the room. "If you're still there. If you still *love* me. Please, Nate!"

To her shock, Nate flinched.

"*Nate!*"

A moment of clarity. He shook his head, managing to meet her gaze. However, it was short-lived, as his eyes grew glassy once more.

"Onward!" Jack instructed.

They moved as one, the cloaked, the afflicted, and the masked. Brother Ascott, Stephen, and Harley obeyed, lifting Charli onto their shoulders as though marching her along her funeral procession. In a way, she supposed they were.

All around them, the sea of afflicted followed. With slow, zombie-like strides, they marched beside her, the bright orange heads of the masked dotted across their number. At the front, Jack danced and skipped, bounding across the grounds, cherishing this freedom. A few times Charli spotted him trip and tumble, before picking himself up with a barking *PAH!* and continuing his merry way into the center of the field. Through her glazed vision, she saw his green aura trailing behind him, leaving patterns in the air.

Charli looked up at the moon, impossibly large, unbelievably orange. Now that she was out in the open, its power flooded down upon her, warming her skin, filling the air with electricity. She couldn't explain it, but she could feel it.

The power.

The aura.

The *magic*.

A magic that defied the laws of nature. A power that had birthed a monster.

A magic that thrummed inside the straw-made creature who was hell-bent on transforming her into his replacement.

Gravity clawed at Charli's ribs, pulling her downward, squeezing tighter with every breathless moment as they righted the crucifix and wedged its tapered bottom into the ground.

Now upright, Charli's head spun. Her eyes adjusted, blinking through the sticky residue of blood and fruity bile. Her heart hammered, breath coming in short, panicked bursts.

In front of her, Jack twirled and danced, arms held wide. The afflicted, masked, cloaked, even the crows in the distance were his audience.

"Yes, my children! Bind her as I was bound. Chain her as I have been chained! Soak it in, my dear! Soon, you will understand my pain and I will understand what it is to be truly free!"

Charli glared at Brother Ascott, securing the fastening at her wrist. Stephen took the other side, carrying out the final checks of their master. Harley, the selfish bitch, placed a stepladder in front of Charli, the cloak protecting her from the globule of spit Charli launched toward the woman.

The anger surged, filling Charli with an unholy desire to scratch, claw, bite, hurt these fuckers who had inflicted this upon the village until they were no more. To unleash all the anger and offense that broiled inside of her and threatened to explode.

If only she wasn't trapped.

"And now, the *final* touch."

Jack vanished in a puff of green smoke, reappearing before her.

Or, *almost* vanishing. Under the heady glow of the orange moon she saw him this time, moving speedily between green cloud bursts, but not able to disappear and reappear like a magician's assistant. Maybe in the dark of the barn, his illusion had carried, but under the watchful eye of the swollen harvest moon, he could not hide his limitations.

Jack clapped his hands. The unspoken command carried through their number, one of the masked ones breaking free of the ranks and dragging an afflicted in turn. They stepped into the open. Charli recognized Alex's clothes. Her jaw tightened as he obediently dragged Julie by his side.

You sick fuck.

Blank-eyed, mouth agape, deep lacerations still leaking on her arms, Julie swayed like a reed in the wind. Behind her, another masked presented her a gift—a hollowed out pumpkin.

Jack beamed. "It's a shame you damaged your last, my dear. But worry not, we've found another that's the perfect fit."

Julie stretched out to hand the pumpkin to Jack. Alex stared blankly ahead, rooted, stoic.

"Oh, no, my love." Jack crooned, eyes flashing. "She's

your friend, isn't she? Perhaps *you* should do the honors. Crown your new queen."

Julie turned without comment, her movements labored and jagged. As she shuffled toward Charli, a *PAH!* tore from Jack's throat, his delight amplified as his green aura swelled and the moon reached its crest. His hands clapped as he danced and whirled around the crucifix, performing full circles around the spot he had guarded for so many years.

Julie moved closer.

Charli strained against her bonds, wrists and ankles on fire as the rough rope scraped her skin. Useless. No escape.

Julie stepped onto the stepladder, came face to face with Charli. The pumpkin rose, outstretched in Julie's bruised, broken hands.

Jack danced on, ignorant and filled with malicious joy.

Julie stared right into Charli's eyes.

And winked.

Charli nearly laughed. She choked it down, and let her head slump. Let the thankful tears fall.

Julie lifted the pumpkin higher, raising it above Charli's head with some struggle.

Jack spun and twisted; a leaf caught in a hurricane. The masked swayed in time with his gleeful cackles.

"You ready, hon?" Julie breathed.

Charli gave a resolute nod.

It all happened so quickly.

Julie dropped the pumpkin beside her.

Thud.

A crack split the side.

Julie reached into Charli's pocket, pulling the short, rusted blade she had stolen from the shed.

Without missing a beat, she hacked at Charli's bonds.

With each frantic saw, the ropes frayed until they finally snapped.

Charli swung like a pendulum, bound only by a single rope. She let out a cry of pain, mirrored by Jack, the sound renting the night.

Jack stopped his dance. His eyes blazed. An unspoken command washed toward his flock.

As one, the villagers took a slow step forward. Then a second. Until it became a shambling march, one by one, two by two, as Jack released a frustrated cry.

"Quickly! Seize them!"

Julie's slicing grew frenzied, the blade cut dangerously close to Charli's skin. With one last wrench, Charli pulled herself free.

She folded. Collapsed to the ground. Her head spun, temples throbbing. She forced herself to stand, her thighs trembling as they adjusted to their sudden freedom, her ankle heavy and swollen.

"Barn!" Charli cried to Julie, seeing the building a short distance away. On her injured ankle she knew she couldn't get far—wouldn't be able to outrun Jack or his followers, but perhaps in there she could barricade herself in. Snatch a moment of reprieve from the monsters.

She broke into a run, the first steps excruciating, but the adrenaline reworking her system soon after. Julie kept pace, only a few steps behind as the building grew larger. Charli's stomach churned. It was the last place she wanted to return to, but what other choice did she have?

Behind her, Julie screamed.

Charli risked a glance back. Julie had fallen. The masked crawled over her like ants on an abandoned sandwich. Around them, the seething crowd of afflicted staggered onward.

Shit. She couldn't stop.

Fuck.

Wouldn't allow her feet to slow.

Julie vanished, her scream the only thing she left behind.

Charli looked back. Nearly lost all control.

By the barn door. Two figures. One robed, one not. One Charli wanted to hurt, harm, destroy. One she wanted to hug, kiss, save.

Harley pulled her hood back, eyes wide and streaming.

"Get inside!"

Charli didn't have time to think. She sped into the safety of the barn as Harley dragged Nate by the wrist and threw him across the straw-strewn concrete. He slid unceremoniously, falling like a limp doll cast from a toddler's hand.

Harley slammed the door shut, securing them inside by sliding a heavy bolt across. She turned to Nate and Charli, then let out a high-pitched yelp as Charli's hand struck her cheek.

TWENTY-NINE

"What the fuck is wrong with you?" Charli barked, anger flushing her sticky cheeks.

Harley started to reply.

Slap!

Another yelp.

Charli's fingers curled into fists, relishing the sense of satisfaction at finally having an outlet for her rage. "What the fuck were you all thinking?"

Harley blinked.

Charli's fist swung, but this time, Harley was ready. Strong fingers wrapped around Charli's wrist. Her strength was impressive as she bent Charli's arm to her waist and twisted, holding her in place as their heads nearly met.

"I've just saved your life, you fucking bitch. How about a thank you?"

Charli laughed. Her first genuine laugh for some time. Behind her, Nate stood, swaying near an idle candle—one of the few sources of light in the musty barn.

"Thank you?"

"That's better." Harley frowned, releasing Charli with a

small shove as though her apology had been genuine. She looked first at Nate, then to Charli. "Are you OK?"

Charli's mouth fell open. "Am I OK?"

Harley rolled her eyes. "This is gonna get real boring, real fast, if I have to keep repeating myself."

Charli growled. "Well, excuse the shit out of me. You're acting like we're friends, like you're not one third of a trio of whackjobs who've just turned an entire town into zombies and unleashed *that* freak of nature. So, it's safe to say, I am *not* fucking OK."

"I *know*!" Harley bellowed back, her cool front suddenly lost as regret colored her face. "You don't think I fucking know that? That I didn't know what we were doing? Well, not fully. I didn't think it would get this bad."

Charli held her arms wide. "What did you *think* was going to happen?"

"They were magic beans, Charli," Harley spat back. "Would you believe it if someone told you that a bag of pumpkin seeds would turn a town's will to your whim? That you could set free an ancient entity that would yield an unlimited bounty? Would you believe it? Would you?"

Nate groaned, stumbling a few steps closer to the candle.

Charli distanced herself from Harley, grabbing Nate's arm to drag him away from the danger of fire.

"Of course I wouldn't," she said. "And even if I did, I wouldn't be dumb enough to risk it. Look what you've done." She turned Nate to face Harley directly, his vacant eyes staring past her from inside his mask. "Look what you've done to my fiancé!"

Charli was surprised to see the emotion that broiled in Harley's face. Compared to the stone-cold bitch she had met the previous day, Harley looked to have broken out of her shell and genuinely seemed to regret what she had helped to ignite.

Something hard crashed against the barn door.

Harley flinched before hopping back and holding the door shut. She pitched her legs before her, digging them into the concrete to brace against another bash against the wood. "You're not the only one who's lost someone, Charli. This might come as a shock, but this isn't all about you."

It was in that moment that Charli realized that it wasn't just her own brother and fiancé who had been affected. Somewhere out there in the pursuing throng were Stacey and Esther, Harley's own friends. Her family were likely out there, too. Although she had played a vital part in making this happen, she was at least trying to make things right.

Even if it may already be too late.

Another crash. Harder this time. Through the small splits in the wooden doors, Charli caught flashes of orange.

She turned to Nate, panicking. "Babe...?"

Nate swayed gently; shoulders drooped.

"Nate... please? It's me. Charli." She grabbed the cheeks of the pumpkin and forced him to face her.

His eyes roamed toward hers, fixing Charli in his gaze from the depths of the pumpkin's shell.

"Chaaar..." He swallowed dryly. "Chaaar..."

"Nate? Nate! Yes... It's me."

"Char... Lee?" Nate struggled with his words, a toddler learning to talk.

"That's right, Charli—"

"Hnghh."

"Babe?"

Charli inched closer. The smell of pumpkin was rank, wafting over her, but she'd been through worse tonight.

Nate took a step closer, then another. As he neared,

Charli noticed a thin crack along the side of the pumpkin's shell, likely made when Harley had hurled him into the barn and he had landed roughly on the concrete. From inside of the gap, spaghetti-thin vines writhed, searching, hunting, reaching. Darting in and out, like worms hiding in the earth.

It's not too late, Charli reassured herself. *It's not too late.*

And then came the others, longer, snaking their way from beneath his sweat-stained collar, the bulge of their passage pressing tight against what remained of Nate's shirt.

Charli's mind flashed back to Kate, strapped to the table. The horrendous scream that had torn from her throat as Harley had made her first incision.

It's only fruit.

Deadly, parasitic fruit...

Shit.

"Babe, I'm going to try something. Do you understand me?"

A flicker of recognition, vanishing in an instant as another thundering crash split the barn.

Harley grunted. "I could do with some help over here."

Shrill laughter from outside. "You can run, but you can't hide! I could play this game *aaaall* night. *PAH! Ha haha hah ha!*"

Another crash

Another.

Coming faster now.

They were running out of time. If they were about to be swallowed by a sea of afflicted and masked, Charli wanted Nate to be with her—the *real* Nate—not this vine-infused monster.

"I'm so sorry, baby. This is going to hurt."

Nate merely grunted as Charli moved behind him. With trembling hands, she dug her fingers beneath the crook of the pumpkin. Sticky, warm, like heated jam. A gentle squelch. Things crawled, attempting to feed on her skin.

Nate screamed. An ungodly sound, his body jerking as the banshee wail erupted from his lips.

Jack fell quiet.

Charli continued, dug deeper, pulled harder. Her heart hammered as she quickly tugged, trying to widen the crack. Small tendrils flailed wildly against her fingers, whipping small welts against the skin as they tried to defend their home. A few latched to her fingertips, feeding hungrily.

Nate's throat grew hoarse from his shrieks. Tears grew hot in Charli's eyes, mixing with Jack's repugnant bile. The fluids mixed, stung, burned. Charli muttered silent prayers as she gripped tightly into the pumpkin, gaining purchase, before tossing herself back against a bale of hay.

Nate sunk to his knees, hands moving to the sides of his head.

The pumpkin segment was hot in Charli's hands, throbbing as though pulsing with its own heartbeat.

A few green worms fell and crawled along the ground.

Nate turned to Charli, the hole in his mask enough to reveal one eye, his nose, and a part of his mouth, the skin as red and raw as campfire embers. His lips were parted, the pain too severe as he fell to all fours and crawled toward her. "Charli! It burns. It fucking burns!"

Charli knelt, helping Nate as his scrabbling fingers worked at the rest of the pumpkin, the two of them in tandem as Nate's shrieks and Charli's sobs combined into a melody that would haunt her until the day she died.

Crash.

Wood panels splintered as Harley watched Nate and Charli in horror.

It was Nate who pulled off the final piece of the pumpkin's mask, his skin left in blotchy patches of orange, green, and red. It was shiny with slime, too, as if he'd spent forty-eight hours beneath water. Where his hair had been were now alopecia patches, some sections as bald as a newborn baby.

Nate finally stopped screaming. He panted in painful relief as he tugged at the last of the tendrils; green cables plugged into his spine. He gasped, chest hitching as he soaked in the relief. Allowed himself a moment of reprieve.

Free.

Crash.

"Guys?" Harley urged.

Charli sniffed, swiping at the snot pouring from her nose, and placed a hand on Nate's shoulder. He leaned into her, still on his knees, resting his forehead against her shoulder. The smell was unbearable, but she couldn't help the relief flooding over her that she had saved Nate.

Hadn't she?

"Nate, are you OK?"

Nate looked up at her, eyes red and bloodshot. His mouth opened. White, pulpy slop poured out, splattering on the ground, his lap, Charli's knees. Charli held him tight, choking back tears as she let it happen, let him release the poison.

And then it was done.

Nate breathed deeply, wiping the residue from his lips. He looked into Charli's eyes. "No, Charli. I'm really fucking not OK."

Despite herself, Charli smiled. Nate gave a weak grin.

Another crash against the door. Harley's voice high as

she fought to brace the doors. "Now that loving reunion is all finished, could one of you give me a fucking hand!"

Charli steeled herself and ran to Harley's side. A few sections of wood had broken free and scattered the floor around them. Through the growing gaps, Charli saw just how many of them there were.

"I don't know how long we can hold them off for, Charli. We need to think of something."

"*PAH!*"

Charli looked for the source of the laughter, her stomach falling. "I don't really think it matters anymore."

All three of them stared upwards at the roof of the barn. Through a small, square hatch, a dark shape crawled inside.

Lithe and large, he sprang down onto the rafters before acrobatically swinging off the beams and landing with a dull *whumpf* in front of them.

"Oh, dear, oh, dear... Little spiders trapped beneath the glass..." Jack stood to his full height, seeming to swell and grow wider as he beamed at them both, the fires within his head raging. "I'm sorry, my lovelies, but playtime's over. The moon is high. It's time to reap the harvest."

THIRTY

J ack stalked toward them. "Years. Years I've waited for this moment, this night. Centuries defending against the carrion, ushering out the vermin... You think you can simply run and hole up in here like a frightened mouse? You are severely misguided..."

Nate rose unsteadily to his feet, arms spread to create a flimsy barrier between Jack and the two women. As he inched back, facing Jack, he stumbled, and Charli worried his legs wouldn't carry him, but he held his position.

"There is no escape, sweetness," Jack said, looking through Nate as if he didn't exist, focusing solely on Charli. "I will be your all, your everything. No one can save you. Not your sibling, not your lover. No one. We *will* trade places, and I..." He let out a long, hearty chuckle, eyes blazing with flame, "I will enjoy being inside you. So warm, so young."

Revulsion spurred Charli's rage. Nate had reached them now, his slime-covered shoulders and head reeking.

"Never!" she cried.

Jack cocked his head. For a moment, the world held its breath.

With a sudden sharp call, Jack declared, "*Now,* my children. Now!"

They were helpless to stop it. Jack's congregation fell against the door. Charli, Harley, and Nate had no choice but to run if they wanted to live.

The barn doors flew open, the wood around the bolt shattering off its moorings. Villagers spilled toward them. Orange orb after bulbous orb stumbled inside, a lumpy, groaning ocean.

Jack's voice called out above the din. "No one can escape, my love! Not even your lover can run from me. I'm inside them all, you see! Safe in the one place you cannot rip out."

To Charli's dismay, Nate shuddered, eyes rolling back in his head. Charli grabbed his wrist and dragged him behind her, but something tunnelled beneath his skin, writhing and crawling, inch by inch, around and around his shoulders, then his neck.

They ducked behind a hay bale large enough to act as a wall to hide from the others. *Not much cover. But it'll do for now.*

Jack cheered on his minions just a short distance away as they flooded the barn.

Nate gagged, and as Charli pulled him closer, a single vine crawled up his throat and protruded from between his lips.

Nate coughed and choked, trying to clear his windpipe.

Without thinking, Charli grabbed the vine and tugged. Nate's eyes filled with tears. The vine was long, but soon whatever root it had found inside Nate came free.

Nate gasped, clutching his throat. He managed a weak, "How many more of them are there going to be?"

"It's time for harvest!" Jack bellowed.

Charli looked out into the barn. They were still flocking inside, blocking each other, bumbling against one another, dozens more still attempting to come in through the front door.

Jack swayed as he orchestrated his slow, steady march. His long arms reached for one of his masked. He ripped the pumpkin off their head, the human beneath crumbling to the ground with a screech. He held the pumpkin toward Charli, waving it back and forth. "A crown for my queen, my sweetness. Don't you want to claim your destiny?"

Charli snarled.

Jack roared with laughter, manic and high-pitched.

Charli tried to flatten herself against the hay. Jack waved the pumpkin back and forth, still cackling. Beside her, Nate gasped for breath. Harley stood a short distance away, bracing herself as the first of Jack's followers rambled around the corner.

Charli's hand rested against her pocket. She ran her fingers over the small lump.

"Nate?" she said softly.

Nate nodded.

She held up Donny's lucky lighter—their last salvation. "Brace yourself. It's about to get hot in here."

Nate offered a weak smile. "I just need you to know one thing, babe."

Charli paused.

"I'm sorry. And, no matter what happens, know that I love you."

Charli couldn't help it, eyes seeing past the fruity pulp. Despite the years of repulsion, despite the events of the last forty-eight hours, all she wanted in that moment was Nate's kiss.

She leaned into him. Their lips touched.

"Come to me, my Harvest Queen," Jack sang, oblivious to their intent.

Nate's eyes hardened as he sank into the hay. "Burn that motherfucker to ash."

Charli held the lighter before her eyes. She thumbed the wheel, catching a spark but no fire. She tried again, and again, and again, even as Harley fought the first of Jack's followers and sent them unconscious to the ground. Even as Jack cackled and sang, danced and provoked. Even as Nate swallowed dryly and urged her on with just a look.

Flick. *Click.*

Flick. *Click.*

Flick. *Click.*

"The Harvest Feast is upon us, my children!"

Jack reached them, towered over them, his eyes surging with infernal flames, the pumpkin raised high above Charli's head.

Charli moaned; thumb numb. She never stopped.

Flick. *Click.*

"Now... Now we enter the age... of *Jack*."

Fwoosh.

Heat. Charli lurched forward, touched the lighter to his elbow.

A spark. Jack was so focused on the mask that he didn't see it. A small ember caught the dry bracken of his body. Charli sank back, watching as Jack danced and spun and laughed.

Another ember, thrown from his thrashing arm, leaped to the nearest hay bale. A thin ribbon of smoke rose as the flame hungrily began its feast.

Jack still hadn't noticed, the pumpkin mask hovering inches above Charli's head.

"My Harvest Queen. Thank you. You will always have my eternal gratitude."

Charli snarled. "Fuck you."

Nate shoved her to one side, letting out an animalistic roar. He sprang at Jack. Tackled him around the waist. Rolled across the ground.

Charli screamed.

Nate punched and pulled, beat and kicked.

Jack threw him off with ease and stood, catching the smile playing across Charli's pale, pinched, pained face.

For a split second, Jack paused.

Charli pointed at his arm. "See you in hell, fucker."

The flames at his elbow grew, catching loose shreds of straw and hay that littered the floor, acting as fuses to the larger stacks nearby.

Jack screeched. "No... *No*! Put it out. Somebody put it out! *No*!"

The flames pulsed. The hay bale erupted, sending smoke and heat high into the air. Fire surged up his shoulder and down his wrists.

All around, the embers magnified, first one stack catching alight, then two, then four, a raging inferno shooting toward the next pile of bone-dry hay, thick clouds billowing, funneling up into the rafters.

Jack staggered back, flapped at the flames, his eyes darting from himself to the bales. His movements only made it worse, helping the embers whirl around in a miniature wind tunnel. "Help. *Help*!"

Poof. He vanished in a puff of gray and green smoke.

Poof. He appeared nearby, the flames only further engulfing his body.

"Babe, come on."

Nate reached for Charli just as a resounding creak rang from above. A timber beam shifted, and before they could move, it fell between them in a wall of fire and wood.

"Nate!"

"Charli! Go! Get out! I'll meet you outside!"

Charli panicked. Everywhere she looked was fire. Everywhere she looked hay was erupting and timber was breaking and creaking. The afflicted and the masked ran in uncoordinated patterns, some crashing into each other, others screeching as fire ate their masks. A few of them simply walked blindly into the inferno, surrendering to their demise as others rolled wildly on the ground.

Somewhere amidst it all, Jack continued his ranting rave, screaming and panicking.

Charli coughed. She had to get out. *Now*.

"Flee!" Jack screamed. "Flee for your lives, my children!"

Charli ran blindly, winding through bodies, skirting past flaming haystacks toward where she hoped the barn doors would be. It was only as she felt the first lick of freedom and fresh air that another figure blocked her path.

Brother Ascott appeared like an apparition, his face a mask of fury. Around him the few lucky villages stalked into the night, the fringes of their clothes alight as they raced for freedom.

"You..." he seethed, teeth gritted and words like poison. "*You—*"

A body crashed into Brother Ascott, sending him sprawling across the concrete. Julie spun, hair wild, face a mask of fear. "Run, Charli. Go!"

"Donny?" Charli asked, but Julie's hands were on her

shoulders, shoving her away, forcing her to move in the direction of the barn doors.

Flames licked the rafters, trailing in strings. Floorboards and beams weakened, cracked, and began to fall.

Somewhere in the middle of it all, Jack screamed, the straw on the floor around his feet alight, flames lunging at his legs, devouring his torso until he was nothing more than a hellish effigy with an orange skull. He thrashed his arms, stumbling wildly in all directions as he only served to spread the fire and crash into his followers who now began to wake and cry out in panic.

Charli cried as she hit a wall, unable to see much else through the smoke.

She prayed—something she'd sworn to never do.

She reached for the meager gaps in the wooden planks that blocked her, wondering if she had any strength left to tear herself free and escape through the wall. But the smoke was too thick, and her lungs were leaden. Each breath was a chore. Each inhale was pumpkin.

Her vision swam.

A figure.

Tall, but not too tall. Muscled, but not heavily so.

The face, familiar.

Charging through the flames, he appeared as an unsteady blur. It was only as his arms scooped beneath her and she found herself lifted that she knew he was real.

"Hold tight, Cee-Cee. We're not done yet."

Charli dipped in and out of consciousness.

Heat.

Darkness.

Thundering footsteps.

Cries of pain.

Skin like melting wax.

Her brother's chest heaving as he carried her to safety.

Cold, cold air.

Alex slowed down as the cool air licked their skin. He was breathless, arms shaking as he eased Charli onto the ground.

She couldn't believe it. She took a long inhale of the clean air, opening her eyes to find the moon staring down at them. Alex's eyes shone.

"Hey, Cee-Cee."

Emotion flooded over Charli. "Alex."

A waxy film covered his face and head. Like Nate, large chunks of his hair had vanished. He reminded Charli of an acid-attack victim, all scars and puckered flesh.

A low laugh pulled from his lips. "Hardly the weekend getaway we wanted, huh?"

She gave him a weak smile in return. "I told you it was a stupid fucking idea."

Creak.

Crack.

They both turned back and watched as the entire left side of the roof collapsed, a shower of angry sparks reaching up to the night. For the first time, Charli noticed that others had escaped into the fields. Dozens of villagers staggered into the fields, coughing and spluttering as they fought to remove their masks.

"Nate?" Alex asked, gaze fixed on the barn.

Charli rose to unsteady feet. "I don't know."

Alex made to run.

"Alex..." Charli warned, but she knew that look in her brother's eyes. She had seen it a thousand times as children, that glint that meant he'd made a decision, and nothing anyone said could change his mind.

Alex paused, turning back to face his sister. "We can't

leave him, Cee-Cee. It's the three of us. It always has been, and it always will be."

Their eyes locked. Time stretched, just for them. Alex nodded. Charli released her grip.

She watched her brother's shape shrink and disappear.

Seconds passed. Minutes.

Then, in the glow, a four-legged figure emerged from the barn. It stumbled, veering left and right with abandon. Charli forced herself to her feet and ran toward them.

"Nate, Alex, here—"

The conflagration swelled.

Boom!

Wood splintered.

Inch-long blades shot in all directions.

A blast of heat, so intense that it stole the last of Charli's strength as she was thrown back.

Her head crunched into the cold, barren earth.

Silence.

EPILOGUE

Restful sleep wouldn't come. Perhaps it never would again.

From the moment she had awoken that morning, she'd known it. Accepted it.

She had assumed the weeks following their escape from Brackenholt might prepare her. Weeks of reminding herself that it was all over, and that he wouldn't be there as her constant source of comfort. Her eternal protector.

The one she'd lost before realising that she wouldn't be able to survive without him.

She'd watched the long mahogany box lower into the ground. Heard the reverend's words. Heard the wails. Had they been hers? She couldn't remember. The knot of hatred had coiled and uncoiled in her stomach, sending her to her knees.

Hands.

Comforting.

Firm.

Pulling her up.

The cold light of an indifferent sun.

The only solace of that day was Nate. He'd stood beside her, watching his best, and only, friend, take his last journey. He'd been there in body, but not in spirit. Charli had avoided his eye contact, and he'd barely registered her questions. He'd only offered a feeble "Hmmm" in response.

Days turned into weeks.

Something had shifted.

They were together, but he wasn't hers. His hairless scalp had recovered first. Before, she'd loved running her fingers through his locks. But now, his hair was short, wiry, severe even. Too short to style and too long to be called "bald." That's what she missed most.

That, and the spark in his eyes. The joy of life.

And his smell.

No matter how much she made him scrub, she could still smell it on him.

A constant reminder of what they'd been.

What they'd lost.

A month later, Nate obediently filled the bathroom with steam and the scent of shower gels, and completed his obligatory scrub until his skin was raw and pink.

She still smelled it.

Oozing from every pore.

It smelled of *him*.

She'd sent Nate back in again.

Charli drew her knees to her chest and closed her eyes. The reassuring hum of idle traffic in the street below grounded her. At her side, her new phone. A new model for a new chapter. At least she could talk to her friends, an easy way to avoid the isolation she couldn't, wouldn't, let herself feel ever again.

Yet, no matter how much she wanted to, she couldn't

bring herself to speak to her girlfriends about what had truly happened.

Couldn't help how many times she'd wondered whether keeping Nate by her side was the right thing to do. She loved him, that much was unquestionable.

But would time heal their wounds? Smooth their scars?

Pain flared in Charli's cheeks. She unclenched her jaw, using her fingers to massage her cheeks. She growled, then eased herself out of bed and toward the window, the edges frosted with condensation from the chill winter winds outside.

Streetlamps turned the fine snowy powder to a buttery glow. Neon lights glared from the nearby corner shop, and someone trailed by on their bicycle, desperately trying not to slip on the ice.

Behind her, Nate emerged from the bathroom, letting out a small, wet cough. Once, twice. She ignored him, and pressed her face to the glass, a soft sigh escaping her lips at the relief of the cold. Fresh air seeped in as she teased the window open, finally clearing away the worst of that noxious scent. She inhaled deeply, then allowed herself to silently cry.

The fields, the moon, the masked, the barn and its flames...

...*Jack.*

Charli jumped back, screaming as his face appeared before her. It leered at her, the bulbous head taking up the window frame, keen eyes burning with wild excitement before—

Charli blinked.

He was gone.

Gentle hands settled on Charli's shoulders. "Hey! Hey... are you OK?"

She didn't turn. Only stared into the soft snowfall. Only saw her own tired reflection staring back.

Nate's warmth spread against her as he wrapped his arms around her waist. She leaned into him, for a moment taking comfort in his presence, until that soft, sweet smell returned.

"It wasn't your fault," he said, his voice gentle.

Charli closed her eyes, shaking her head. "It is. I should have stopped him..." She swallowed hard, the words catching in her throat. "I'm sorry, I didn't mean it like—"

"I know."

"He was my brother, Nate. He saved us, and because of us—"

"Stop." His arms tightened around her. "Alex chose. He always did. He wouldn't want it any other way. He..." Nate let out a sad sigh. "He loved us both, and I wish he was still with us. But if he hadn't done what he did, more would have died. It's not fair. None of it is. But that's what happened and..." He pressed his face into Charli's shoulders. "I love you."

Charli paused. "I know."

At that moment, it was enough.

As Nate wept against her skin, she stared into the window again. The street was still, the snow blanketing everything in white. Somewhere in the gloom she imagined thatched houses, a far-off field, and a scarecrow.

More coughs.

Nate stepped back, hacking into the ring of his fist, the burst so suddenly urgent that for the first time in forever, Charli looked at him with concern. "Are you OK?"

Nate nodded, coughing again. He patted his chest with a fist, clearing his throat. "Yeah. Just phlegm. It's cold, y'know?"

Despite her hesitations, Charli stepped close and planted a small kiss on Nate's lips. "Time to rest, yeah?"

"Yeah."

They climbed back into bed together, back-to-back.

No sleep.

No rest.

Again.

Charli thought of all the villagers who'd perished, the fire engines that arrived far too late. When the waters had eventually doused the last of the flames, the greenest of the fire crew vomited. Dozens of charred bodies beneath the wreckage. The lucky few, skin still slick with pulp, had helped, claiming their dead.

Charli wondered whether there would be enough of them left to keep the village going.

She hoped not.

Some traditions deserved to die.

Charli fought the sleep. Sunlight peeked over the horizon, the soft orange glow warmed the room, and the suburbs woke for the day.

Nate coughed again. Rolled over.

Charli got up. He needed a drink. She grabbed a glass and shuffled to the kitchen. As she turned back, her feverish mind conjured images of fields.

Of harvests.

Of seeds.

Like the one that Nate held out toward her, eyes wide, orange-tinged bile dribbling down his chin.

YOUR NEXT READ...

AN EXCLUSIVE PREVIEW OF YOUR NEXT TWISTED TALES STORY

YOU'VE SEEN WHAT GROWS IN THE FIELDS. NOW COME MEET WHAT HOWLS IN THE DARK.

Start **your next nightmare** with a sneak peek at *Heir*, the second standalone horror in the *Twisted Tales* series.

ORDER YOUR COPY NOW

TWISTEDTALESBOOKS.COM/HEIR

Or visit www.twistedtalesbooks.com to see our growing library of horrors...

TWISTED TALES

HEIR

HOWLEY &
WILLCOCKS

PROLOGUE

— 1991 —

That night, Lydia dreamed of dogs.

Not the cute kind. Not chihuahuas, terriers, cockerpoos, or labradors.

No.

That night, Lydia dreamed of wolves.

"Mama, help," she screamed, racing through the dark forest, trees whipping by on either side. The ground uneven, each step a gamble on her ankles. They were right behind her. Just out of reach. But close enough to hear their growls, smell their dank fur. Feel the heat of their hungry breath.

Her cloak flashed in the silver moonlight, a red blur as it snapped around her shoulders. Her mind returned to the story Mama had read that night. Pages filled with a little girl and the hungry wolf that ate her grandmother...

"Mama! Help me!"

She saw it ahead of her, through the break in the trees that would not come closer. She was on a treadmill, the manor statue-still ahead beneath the full moon, Flopsy's plush rabbit ears dangling and flopping in the crook of her arm.

She reached out.

Flopsy fell.

Vanished into the night.

Something gripped at Lydia's dress. Tugged it sharply.

A triumphant howl and—

—"Wake up, *now*. We need to go."

"Mama, what's happening?"

Fingers. Nails. Digging into her skin. Her whole body moved as she rose from sleep into darkness and panic.

"Darling. Up. *Now*."

Grown-up hands gripped her childish frame. Lifted her from the bed, pulled Lydia from the warm cocoon of her sheets into the ever-cold of the manor. Her bare feet tensed on chilled stone tiles as she was placed upright and unsteady, eyes fighting to adjust to the gloom.

"This way."

Her mother's grip was a vice on her wrist. As she was dragged into the hallway, she was vaguely aware of the others. Eyes reflecting the moonlight cast through the large, chiseled windows. Her siblings. Each of them wary and staring, looking up and down the hall.

Deep in the belly of the manor, something growled.

"All of you. Follow me." Her mother held her arms out for the youngest, a girl still swaddled in baby blankets. The oldest and tallest of them, eight years old with dark hair and eyes wide, handed over the bundle, uttering a weak protest. "Mom...What's..."

"*Now*."

"I don't..." the second eldest tried.

"*Enough!*"

Their mother spun away, stepping towards the open

window. Lydia didn't know what time it was, but she knew it was late. The moonlight limned their mother, high-lighting her wild hair, the deep grooves under her eyes, reflecting a fear that would haunt Lydia until her dying day. The baby stirred. "There's no time. We have to..."

A singular, howling note rent the night. Feral. Primal. Enough to cause the baby to cry. For the three children to huddle together, their breath stolen, hearts galloping.

In years to come, Lydia would recall that moment, that singular beat of a second where their mother deflated. Where her tears welled, and her mouth drooped on either side. It was the moment Lydia understood true fear. The moment that childhood ended, and her running began.

"*RUN!*"

They did. The two boys sprinted down the hallway, feet beating a drum march against stone. Their mother grabbed Lydia's wrist once more, dragging her forward even as she juggled the baby in the crook of her other arm. Through the labyrinth of the manor's hallways, spurred on by the impossible howls. Howls that neither grew nor faded. Howls that seemed to come from the walls themselves.

Down the stairs to the second floor, past the statues and oil paintings of their ancestors. Bare feet slapping across long, ornately woven rugs that kicked up faint puffs of dust with each frenzied step.

Down again to the first floor, a short run to the next flight of stairs. The boys were already ahead, guided by panic and a desire to save themselves.

Tears blurred Lydia's eyes. The baby roused, complaining and gurgling against their mother's thumping heart. It was only as they made it down the final flight and into the foyer of the grand manor that they heard it.

The silence.

Lydia let out a small squeak. "Mama..."

"Shhh." Her mother searched the foyer, until her breath shuddered and died.

"No."

Lydia saw them.

Stalking down the hallway.

Two violet eyes.

Two rows of glistening teeth.

A nightmarish creature, twisting in and out of the shadows.

Lydia barely had time to register the shape before her mother grabbed the back of her head, pressing Lydia's face into her chest. Barely felt the quick kiss on her forehead. Barely gripped the wriggling bundle that was forced into her arms.

But she heard her mother's scream.

The creature's frenzied roar.

The doors groaned open, the two boys calling out in panic. Lydia was manhandled, thrown into the cold air that licked her skin with a frosty tongue. It took everything she had to hold the baby steady. Keep her safe.

The baby wailed. The doors slammed shut behind her. Hands, helping Lydia up, taking the baby.

Not her mother. Couldn't have been Mama.

Because Mama was screaming. Bloodcurdling terror and pain.

Lydia knew this to be true, even as the screams shrank into silence.

Even as the four small figures escaped across the lawn, heading toward the forest.

Even as they crested the top of the hill a short while later, and looked down upon the nearby town, only a few buttery lights glinting in curtained windows.

Even as they sank to the ground, clutching each other tight, their minds caging away the memory of that violet-eyed demon. And, as the years blurred by, so too would the memories. The greatest, and most important memory to be forgotten, would be the promise that Lydia made to herself as the four of them approached the town under the golden glow of the rising sun, eyes red and blotchy from the tears that wouldn't stop.

The promise that she made to herself never to return to...

CHAPTER
ONE
— 2006 —

...olfridge Manor.

Lydia shuddered. It already seemed like a lifetime ago that the cab had dropped her off on the far side of the woods, the driver giving her a deep look of concern before he sped back to town. With each step along the trailing mud path that led through the pine forest, she wished she hadn't come.

Wished she'd made better life choices.

Wished she was still at home in her stuffy apartment.

But she hadn't, and she wasn't.

The sun was high, casting its rays on the manor grounds, much to the delight of the early blooming wildflowers on the unkempt lawn. Around the edges of the old stone building, Monarch butterflies, hoverflies, and fuzzy carpenter bees darted around the flowers and fragrant shrubs.

In the center of the gravel drive was a feature set apart from the main building. An ancient stone fountain. Several stone wolves were hewn across its three tiers, with strings of moss and lichen hanging from their faded jaws like moldy drool.

Was that working the last time I was here?

Swiping a tattooed arm across her forehead, Lydia tried to process the uncomfortable feeling that settled in the pit of her stomach.

She had next to no memory of this extraordinary place. Couldn't remember the east and west wings that stretched around her like the arms of a giant's embrace. Couldn't recall the tangles of ivy that ran over the ornate stonework. Had no recollection of the multiple stories of the building, and the immense front garden complete with pebble stone drive.

The only thing she did remember was the little voice inside her head which told her to—

—*Run!*—

—get far, far away from here. And the fact that once, oh so very long ago, this had been her family home.

Lydia reached into her back pocket, drawing out the aged parchment envelope with a crimson wax seal. She'd cracked the seal but could still make out the family crest in the imprinted circle. Two wolves baying at a full moon with a dagger piercing its center.

Fifteen years...

It had been fifteen years since...

"Are you gonna stand out there all day staring or are you gonna give your baby sis a hug!"

Lydia started, looking up to the thin sash windows directly above the large oak front doors. Emily Wolfridge, all red curls and even, white teeth, waved enthusiastically.

Lydia stared up, unable to smile, unable to reply. Suddenly her clothes felt too tight against her skin, the sun too warm.

Emily rolled her eyes. "Fine. I'll come down to you. Wait there. Don't move!"

Lydia adjusted the straps of her canvas backpack. Cracked pins and faded band badges decorated the front, the bag light and only half full thanks to her modest packing.

She didn't plan on staying long.

Not if she could help it.

The doors flew open. A rush of warm air wafted from inside the manor, as though the building had just belched. Her nose wrinkled. A scent that Lydia didn't recognize— sharp, unfamiliar, and wrong. Every hair on her arm stood on end.

"It's *so* good to see you!" Emily wrapped her arms tightly around Lydia's neck.

Emily was at least a foot shorter than Lydia, with keen green eyes that sparkled in the sun. She smelled of lilacs and lilies and, despite her misgivings, Lydia yielded to the embrace.

"Gosh!" Emily stepped back. "I can't believe you're here. James said you wouldn't come. I told him he was just being stupid. How long's it been?"

That was a question Lydia didn't want to answer. Because answering meant acknowledging something that, for the last few years, she'd ignored with steadfast determination. The knowledge that her formative years had been fundamentally different to her siblings. In her other life, she was free. In this one, all it had taken to bring her back to her broken family was a piece of faded yellow parchment, some fountain pen cursive, and a wax seal.

Luckily for Lydia, Emily didn't get a chance to press for an answer.

"Give her a moment to breathe, won't you?" a voice

called from the top steps, the figure standing in the shadow of the open front door. "She's only just arrived. I imagine she wants to scrub off the journey, isn't that right?"

At first, she didn't recognize him. Puberty had hit James like a steam train, and the acne-ridden teenager who she'd once enjoyed screaming matches with during the midnight hours had blossomed into a fine young man. Gone were his wet-look gelled spikes and glasses, and in place was neatly combed hair and diamond blue eyes. He'd even thrown out his tattered denim jacket, replacing it instead with a short-sleeved plaid shirt, complete with a hood.

If she didn't still see him as her awkward teenage brother, she might have thought a catalogue model had taken his place.

James sensed Lydia's trepidation, holding out his arms as he examined himself. Something gold flashed on one of the fingers of his left hand. "I know. I look a little different, huh? Then again, you're not exactly as I last remembered you. Nice ink. When did you get those?"

Lydia shrugged. "Over the years."

"I *love* what you've done with this," Emily said, reaching into Lydia's personal space and pinching a blonde stripe that flowed through her chestnut locks.

Lydia pulled her head back, tucking the stripe behind her ear. "Thanks." She looked past Emily to James. "Nice ring. Who's the lucky lady?"

His cheeks flushed and his eyes hardened. "Don't be a bitch. His name's Cory."

A soft smile curled Lydia's lips, a gentle warmth blossoming inside her chest. She met James's gaze, the two of them exchanging a full, unspoken conversation before Lydia cleared her throat. "And what about the other one? Is it just us three, or are we going to be graced by his existence today?"

A strange look passed between Emily and James.

"What?" Lydia asked.

"We don't know," James answered, standing awkwardly.

"What do you mean you don't know?"

Emily batted away a bright yellow butterfly, "We figured that if he was going to reach out to any one of us, it would've been you."

"Me?"

Emily smirked, though the humor didn't reach her eyes. "You're the dynamic duo that ran away."

Lydia's brow furrowed. "But doesn't he *need* to be here though? Doesn't this involve all of us? Isn't that the whole point of this wildcard reunion? If he doesn't come, what happens?"

James shrugged. "We don't know."

They stood in pregnant silence for a long moment. Somewhere far in the distance, a lone police siren wailed. The only sign that civilization existed outside of the grounds of the manor.

James took a deep breath, composing himself as he plastered on a practiced smile. "Look, until we know what he's doing, why don't you drop your stuff in your room? We're all stuck here until this is over, so we may as well get comfortable. Plus, you must be exhausted from your trip from..."

Lydia didn't answer, already sensing that James was trying to bait the location of her home from her.

James chuckled. "Worth a shot. Follow me."

Emily skipped up the steps behind James. Her energy made Lydia grin as she watched, not quite believing that this was the young sister she had left all those years ago. While James had grown up, Emily was still filled with that joyous naivety that came with youth. Oh, to be sixteen again.

Soon the world would kick that hope to the curb and she'd have to grow up.

Until then...

The oak doors banged shut behind them. The temperature dropped several degrees. The air inside the manor was thick, almost tangible with neglect and age. The marble floor was cracked. Each step they took echoed through the cavernous space. Faded tapestries hung limply from the walls, their stories lost to dust and decay.

"Remember how we used to race down these halls?" James's voice was a welcome distraction, his gaze wandering the building as he lost himself to his own memory. "We'd have our arms out like we were airplanes."

He stepped towards Lydia and grabbed her wrists, starting to pull them up. He winked and wriggled an eyebrow.

Lydia bristled and pulled back. "Don't you fucking dare."

James dropped his arms and went into a fake slump.

"Besides, how could I remember? I was three years old."

"What *do* you remember?" Emily asked.

"Nothing good." She looked to James.

James's smile slipped. "Only the good times. Then... nothing."

That makes three of us.

They passed beneath a chandelier hanging precariously from the ceiling, half its crystals missing. With each detail she noticed, Lydia's shoulders bowed, forced down by the weight of hundreds of years of memories and unseen eyes.

Emily stared open-mouthed around the space. "I cannot believe we used to live here. This place is *huge*."

James guided Lydia up a grand staircase, their footsteps muffled by the violet and gold carpet cascading down the stone steps. The next landing was just as opulent, with hallways sweeping off in multiple directions. Instead of chandeliers, sconces lined the walls, flickering with weak electricity inside dust-lined cases. Statues lined the walls, great stone things of regal men, each as different as the last. Except for the carved wolves sitting beside them, each stone pet almost identical.

Despite herself, Lydia kept glancing over her shoulder, expecting to see eyes watching her. In the back of her mind was a low-level snarl that she couldn't shake away.

"I know it seems gloomy, but I don't think we'll be staying long," James said, watching Lydia without her realizing. "As far as I'm aware, we meet the lawyer, sign what we need to sign, and agree what needs to be agreed. I'm not sure why the letter said to bring an overnight bag, but whatever is going on we'll be done by morning." He paused, his expression softening. "If staying here is too much for you, I saw a bar in town that supposedly does good food. They've got a pool table and darts too, so if you wanted to hang for a little bit before we—"

"I've got things to get back to."

Emily and James exchanged a look.

"Right," James said. "OK."

They passed by more doors than Lydia could keep track of. By the time they reached the third floor, the air was so cold that she had to roll down her sleeves to keep warm. The only thing that kept her pressing forward was her curiosity of seeing her childhood bedroom for the first time in over a decade.

"Just up here," James said. "Amit gave us a short tour when we arrived—at least to the main function rooms. Emily and I didn't go in. We figured you'd want to be the first to see it. Y'know… Memories and all that."

"Who's Amit?"

"Don't be rude. It's *Mr Singh*," Emily said. "You're gonna meet him soon enough. He's in the dining room with all the papers. Told us to join once we were all here. Seems nice enough. Hard to get a good read of—"

"Emily, *watch out!*"

James darted in front of his sisters, arms spread wide.

A dark shape appeared, glimpsed like a strobe in the flickering lights.

Cold, calculating eyes.

Lydia gasped.

Memories.

Ripping, tearing teeth.

Monstrous howls.

Their mother's screams.

Like what you've read so far? Want to read more? Continue your adventure at www.twistedtalesbooks.com…

AUTHOR NOTES

BY DANIEL WILLCOCKS

I still remember the very moment that the Twisted Tales series was born.

It doesn't happen often, but when a powerful idea strikes, it affects the entire body. Skin tightens. Heart pounds. Adrenaline pumps.

Sounds a lot like fear, doesn't it?

Yet excitement, while it presents the same, is far more powerful.

I was walking through Swanholme Park in Lincoln, skirting the lakes, basking in the sun, when the idea hit me:

What if there was a series that was basically *Goosebumps for adults?*

It seemed so simple. Stine's *Goosebumps* series captured my childhood. I loved those tales: short snippets of horror in collectible books that were powered by a twisted imagination.

I remember cameras that took pictures of people's deaths. Lizard people. Haunted dummies.

MONSTER BLOOD.

Shudder.

But in the several decades since my childhood, I had yet to see anything that even came close to giving me that horror-laced experience.

So, why not make it yourself? said the voices in my head.

That was in the summer of 2021. Under the shade of a large oak, birds chirping, and insects buzzing, it came to me in flashes. I recorded a voice note to send to my partner at the time, detailing everything that has now become the Twisted Tales you hold in your hands.

And that's where it sat.

That's where it waited.

Ideas are very much like seeds. They take their sweet time as they root in the soil. For years you think that nothing will grow, and then suddenly the first sprout springs from the ground.

That was when Rob (R.P. Howley) joined in.

Now, a quick side tale for those who may not know Rob that well.

Rob is a powerhouse.

In 2024, I co-edited an anthology of flash fiction with Samantha Frost. For this anthology, we received hundreds of submissions which we read anonymously so that we could whittle down the list of final entries for the book without bias of names we might know.

When we selected our finalists and unveiled the names of those who would have stories included in the book, Rob had seventeen stories to be included.

Seventeen, of eighty(ish).

Rob is almost too good of a writer, and it's his strengths that balance out my weaknesses in writing a series like this. Where I'm sometimes too flowery with language, Rob simplifies. Where Rob sometimes skips over description and emotion, I provide the heart of the arcs.

It's a symbiotic relationship that just works.

It was around the time of the anthology that became "Bolts of Fiction" that I reached out to Rob and asked if he wanted to join forces with me on this little series idea that wouldn't leave me the f**k alone.

And, thus, Twisted Tales blossomed.

The book you're holding in your hands is evidence of a vision turned reality. It's a testament to a working relationship that combines graft, grit, and fun. "Jack" is only the beginning of the Twisted Tales series.

Whether this is your first book, or the tenth that you've read, know that no matter when you're reading this we're already working hard on the next Twisted Tales book.

Because this is what we love. We love horror. We love entertaining readers. And we cannot get enough of the fact that readers are enjoying this series and providing amazing reviews and generous feedback.

That's the beautiful thing about writing. Each time I sit down at the keys to work on the latest version of a Twisted Tales story, I think back to that sunny day in Lincoln.

Blue skies.

Blue water.

Thumping heart.

Sweating forehead.

Body shaking.

Because whether it's fear or excitement that's got us trembling, one thing is definitely for certain...

...it's all for you, Dear Reader.

— Daniel Willcocks
25 June, 2025

P.S. I wanted to take a quick moment to extend some thanks to the people who contributed to the creation of this book.

Firstly, to Rob for being an invaluable writing partner and helping shape what this book has become. Long may the Twisted Tales pen run with ink.

Luke Kondor, for his constant inspiration, motivation, and support with each book, story, or idea that springs into my brain.

Samantha Frost, who endured countless hours of conversations and voice notes in the early days of this series' inception, and kept the flames alive on this project.

All of the writers who I speak to on the regular and who pave the way for better fiction: Gemma Amor, Neil McRobert, Ally Wilkes, Sam Rebelein, Dan Howarth, Dan Soule, and those whose names escape me in this moment, but who know the impact you have.

100covers.com for the incredible cover art.

And, most of all, to you Dear Reader, for making it all the way to the end of the book and enduring the credits in the hope of a Marvel post-credits scene.

I'm sorry to disappoint. While we have no extra scene, we do have a free story to give. Just turn the page and see for yourself...

JOIN THE TWISTED TRIBE

What's that? We're still not done?

How do you fancy getting your hands on a **FREE SHORT STORY**, as well as joining a band of Twisted superfans all benefiting from exclusive discounts, behind the scenes news, and more?

Join the Twisted Tribe and join Dan and Rob on their mission to build the largest community of horror readers on the planet.

There are so many ways to get involved, but here are the easiest ones for you:

CLAIM YOUR FREE STORY AT TWISTEDTALESBOOKS.COM

JOIN OUR ONLINE DEVIL'S ROCK COMMUNITY

discord.gg/vbbCrkQ6Pf

LEAVE A REVIEW

Reviews are the lifeblood of your favorite authors. Consider leaving a review on Goodreads, as well as your preferred purchase platform.

ABOUT THE AUTHORS

Robyn Howley has three requirements to function; black coffee in the morning, red wine in the evening, and writing in between. He has the imagination of a six-year-old, the soul of a retiree, and dreams of one day making a full time income as a multi-passionate creative.

He currently lives in Portsmouth, England, and when he's not writing, he's nestled on his favourite reading chair, wine in hand, consuming books; podcasts and YouTube tutorials on all aspects of writing, publishing and entrepreneurship.

He also designs notebooks and blank journals as Whitscribe Jotter, which are currently available for sale on Amazon.

Find out more at www.rphauthor.com
www.instagram.com/robynhowleyauthor
www.facebook.com/robynhowleyauthor

Daniel Willcocks is an international bestselling author and award-winning podcaster known for his dark fiction. He is the founder of Devil's Rock Publishing, co-founder of the chart-topping fiction podcast The Other Stories, and host of The Writer's Chair podcast.

Since 2015, Daniel has written or ghostwritten over 70 books, spanning horror, speculative fiction, and beyond. He is endlessly fascinated by the power of storytelling—and committed to building bold, immersive worlds that linger long after the final page.

Find out more at www.danielwillcocks.com
www.instagram.com/willcocksauthor
www.facebook.com/willcocksauthor
bsky.app/profile/danielwillcocks.bsky.social

More from Howley & Willcocks

Twisted Tales Series

Jack

Heir

Slay

Deal

R.P. Howley

Welcome to Eldmere: A Horror Anthology

Lingering Curses:: A Horror Anthology

Find more at www.rphauthor.com

Daniel Willcocks

Dream

The Omens Call

The Other Side

They Rot (Book 1 of "The Rot" Series)

Twisted: A Horror Anthology

When Winter Comes

Find more at www.danielwillcocks.com

Keep up-to-date at

www.devilsrockbooks.com

www.ingramcontent.com/pod-product-compliance
Lightning Source LLC
Chambersburg PA
CBHW032120170626
46808CB00006B/2029